MW01286519

Tower of the Dead
Ray Wenck

Copyright © 2016 Ray Wenck
Editor: Jodi McDermitt
Cover: Ren McKinzie
Published by: Glory Days Press

Dedication
This work is dedicated to zombie apocalypse survivors
everywhere.
And to Jon Wenck for talking me into it.

Acknowledgments

I never started out to write a zombie story. My interest is in dystopian, non-zombie, post-apocalyptic worlds. However, after complaining to my son, Jon, about having numerous potential readers at various comic cons put a book down because it didn't have zombies, he said, "Well, write a zombie story, then." So I did, and actually had fun doing it. He was the first person to read it and gave it a thumbs up. Depending on the success of this one, I already have a sequel in mind.

As with any project like this, there are always many people to thank. First, my editor, Jodi McDermitt of Grammar and Tonic. Next, the awesome artist responsible for this amazing cover, Ren McKinzie.

I would like to thank Nancy Kueckels-Averill, RN, BSN, for always being there to help with medical questions. I would also like to send out a special thank you to Nancy Talbot for being a saving angel and helping a complete stranger during a difficult time. You will always have a warm place in my heart, Nancy.

Thanks again to John Remmer for all his help with my printing needs.

Lastly, to my readers, thank you. Without you, I could not do what I do. I appreciate your support and love hearing your comments at comic con signings and the reviews you post online. Keep it up.

1

"You sure you know where you're going?"

The thin man said, "Yeah, no sweat."

Yet pouring sweat was what he did, profusely.

The tug bumped against the long-abandoned pier, taking both men by surprise, forcing staggered steps sideways to catch their balance. The tugboat captain, a heavy bald man with a full black and gray beard, set the throttle to idle. In the darkness he was forced to travel the river in, he hadn't judged the pier's distance into the water very well.

The tug settled, but the long flat top barge he hauled behind bumped and drove the tug forward. The two men waited, wondering if the sound had been heard, not fearing the human element as much as the other deadlier creatures that now existed in this strange world. The captain listened intently while his first and only mate prepared for his mission. The only sound that came to him was the steady hum and buzz of the insects. It didn't matter that the world had changed; that sound never did. Insects survived no matter what befell the human race.

He turned his attention to the mate, feeling an apprehensive chill tickle his spine. "Can you do this alone? I mean, how much can you actually carry to make this worthwhile?" He wanted the treasure they sought; wanted it very badly, but not at the cost of his life.

His first mate smiled. "Don't worry. Even one case of this stuff will get us a great price."

The captain nodded. He glanced around nervously, trying to pierce the darkness that engulfed them. They ran without lights. They couldn't risk discovery from denizens on either side of the wide river.

He nodded. "Okay. But I can't wait for long. They'll be expecting us back in an hour and a half. That only gives you an hour to get there and back."

"Don't worry. I'll be back in time. If we're a few minutes late, we'll just say we went farther out this time."

The captain rubbed his jowly face. "But-but what if you run into—you know?"

The first mate lifted his sweat-soaked shirt and patted the butt of the gun stuck in the waist of his pants. "I've got protection."

The tug rocked slightly as its own wake bounced back from the shoreline. The thin man jumped to the ancient wooden pier and disappeared into the blackness.

"Be careful," the captain called after him in a whispered voice.

The captain reached into his pocket and withdrew the small flask he'd found on the garbage pile during one of his trips. He'd cleaned it inside and out, and it had become his constant companion. He lifted it to his lips and swallowed twice. "Ah!" Swirling the container, he frowned. Not much left. Should he save it? He looked to the shore. Nah! If what Malcolm said was true, he'd soon have plenty to refill it with. Smiling, he tipped the flask up again and drained the contents.

While screwing the cap back on, the barge bounced underneath him. He swore and glanced back into the darkness. "Damn!" he muttered. The platform must have drifted and hit the shore. He prayed he hadn't gone aground. An involuntary shudder ran the length of his body. As much as he wanted to score from Malcolm's find, waiting scared the shit out of him. He wanted very much to turn on the engine and the lights, but knew all too well what the sound and brightness might draw. Another shiver ran through him, raising gooseflesh and making him wish he had saved a little of the whiskey. He desperately needed another drink. He swatted at a bug and cursed louder than intended.

The barge bounced and swayed several more times. His fear grew. The captain began to pace the deck. They had planned out this excursion for several days. His job was to haul the island's refuse out to sea once a week. He was supposed to go far enough out in open water to ensure the garbage buildup would not create a problem. Tonight he had shortened that trip, only reaching the mouth of the river before dumping his load.

The time ticked away with agonizing slowness. He checked his watch. Malcolm had been gone far too long, yet it had only been a little more than twenty minutes. What if he hadn't made it? He hated the thought of finishing the trip dry. He gave little thought to Malcolm's safety. He could always find another first mate. Losing a large cache of booze and the profits it would bring, though; that he would mourn.

Almost an hour later, the captain's patience and courage had about run out. The platform continued to bob, adding to his anxiety. He couldn't see past the end of the tug, but the constant bouncing of the deck beneath him had him spooked. His imagination created all sorts of horrifying scenarios. He was about to say *fuck it* and fire up the engines when he heard a crash along the shore. His heart leaped to his throat. Not sure if it was Malcolm or one of the crits, the captain risked using the flashlight he kept under the wheel to be sure.

The light flared and fell across a fast-moving man carrying a cardboard box. The man froze.

"Turn off that fucking light," Malcolm said. "I think some of them are following me."

That thought sent a spear of fear through the captain. He flicked the light off and hastened from the cabin to help his first mate. The man stepped off the shoreline onto the rickety wooden pier. The captain stretched over the gunwale, taking the box, while Malcolm untied the line. The captain set the box down inside the cabin and began checking the contents. A heavy thump told him Malcolm had made it on board.

"Is this it?" the captain said, pointing at the box.

"What do you mean, 'Is this it?' Isn't that enough? How the fuck was I gonna carry any more than that?"

"I was only asking if there was any more. If you were going back. Staying here for this long is giving me the willies."

"That's it, for now. Let's go."

The captain bent to move the box, but Malcolm said, "I'll see to that, you just get this tub moving."

The captain hesitated, looking from Malcolm to the box of booze. He rubbed a hand over his mouth, desperately needing a drink, then turned and moved as fast as his chunky legs would go to the wheel. The engine coughed and sputtered, and for a frightening moment, he feared the old tug wouldn't start. But then it caught, and relief flooded over him. Now, if only he wasn't hung up on any rocks. He held his breath until the vessel began to move.

The captain turned to watch Malcolm, and to his annoyance, saw the man count the bottles. What did the man think, that he would steal a bottle? There hadn't been enough time. As Malcolm stood, he lifted a bottle of Jameson's with a bright smile on his face. The sight of the bottle wet his mouth and the annoyance and nervousness of the past hour dissipated. "Well, go on. Pop it open. Let's have a taste."

"We have to decide whether we want to drink it or sell it. I've got cheaper bottles of whiskey in here we can drink, but this is the only bottle of Jameson's there was. You know how much old man Welsh will pay for this?"

Greed battled thirst as the captain's mind ran through the two options. With a sigh, greed won. "Open one of the cheaper ones." The price he could get for that one bottle would see him in cheaper booze for a month.

"I thought that's how you'd see it." He replaced the Jameson's and pulled out a cheaper brand of whiskey. Twisting the cap, he took a long pull, finishing with an, "Ahhh! Heaven!" He passed the bottle to the captain, who wiped the opening on his dirty shirt and took an even longer swallow. Then he pulled out the flask and attempted to fill it.

"Hey, careful. You're spilling some. There's not that much more to get."

The captain stopped and looked at his mate. "You mean there's more where you got this?"

Malcolm nodded with suspicious caution. "Yeah, probably

enough for three more cases, but I'm the only one who knows where it is," he added hastily.

"What kinda stuff?"

"Mostly cheap, but at this point, that doesn't matter. Booze is so scarce, anything will bring top dollar."

That thought brought a smile to the captain's craggy face. With the money and notoriety he would get from the sale, he planned on petitioning for a room in the tower. His mind wandered. Better accommodations, better food, women, and rubbing elbows with the elite. His dream was interrupted by Malcolm. "Hey, stop hogging the whiskey."

Reluctantly, the captain handed it back, then turned his attention to his course. The island's southern docks were not far away. He needed to cross the current and get to the other side of the river now, or it would be too late. They would sail past them. He hated having to turn around and try to dock from the other direction.

His concentration occupied, he forgot all about the booze. Ten minutes later, the dim bulb over the dock, his lone point of reference, came into view. Above the water, a series of dim bulbs lit the bridge, the only connection between the mainland and the island. If he reached that point, he had gone too far. He adjusted course a bit and slowed the tug's speed. Soon, the outline of the dock was clear. It jutted out about twenty yards from shore.

He turned to see Malcolm with the bottle nearly half empty, sitting on the floor, fondling the other bottles.

"Jesus Christ, cork that bottle and get ready to dock."

The man looked up through glazed eyes, already half in the bag. "Now, you worthless ..." He left the rest to drift off. Malcolm replaced the bottle in the case and got to his feet. He held on to the side wall for a moment to steady himself, then saluted and left the cabin to ready the lines.

The captain envisioned the fool falling between the boat and pier and getting crushed. His first thought was *good*; he wouldn't have to share the profits, but then he remembered Malcolm had said there were three more cases. No, he couldn't lose his trusted first mate yet.

He throttled back and the engines changed pitch. In the faint light, he saw Malcolm jump to the dock, hauling the line. It would've been nice if that lazy ass Smulders was down here to catch the line and tie them off, especially since that was his job. If he thought he was going to get some of the valuable booze, he could forget it. Maybe next time, he'd hustle his fat ass down from the comfort of his little shed and help them dock instead of making Malcolm do it on his own.

Malcolm tied off the bow with expert efficiency, then moved to tie off the second line. With a satisfied smile, the captain shut the engine down. He turned to the box of booze, found the open bottle and pulled it out. Twisting the cap free, he pulled out his flask and once again went about filling it, his concentration so focused, he ignored the thump on the deck of the tug. It was only Malcolm returning. Finished with his task, he capped the flask and licked his hand of the whiskey that dripped there, then lifted the bottle for another drink.

As the bottle touched his lips, he became aware of a body coming toward him. He gulped fast, not wanting to hear Malcolm's complaints about him drinking more than his share. A few drops found their way into his airway and he coughed. He extended the bottle toward Malcolm and turned his head to cough some more.

Malcolm grabbed the bottle, then his hand. By the time the captain found the action curious and looked, the hand of the crit was now wrapped around his arm, pulling it toward its half-missing mouth. Panic exploded in his chest. His scream ended in still another cough. He pulled back, but the decrepit arm held tight. Then a second form emerged from behind the first, then a third. This time, he did scream. The bottle hit the deck and burst open. The smell of whiskey wafted upward.

He managed to snake his arm free from the first crit, but fire ran up his arm. He'd been scratched. He tried to flee, but tripped over the case of booze. He fell, and before he could rise again, they fell upon him, smothering his cries of pain and for help. Teeth bit into him, ripping his flesh from his body. In the distance, he was vaguely aware of another scream, not his, and understanding its source, knew all hope for a rescue was gone.

The pain numbed as more creatures came to the feast. His vision clouded, narrowed, and disappeared. His last conscious thought was of needing a drink.

2

Evan Stewart sat on the plush sofa, listening politely to the story his host was telling. In the back of his mind, one thought swirled in continuous motion: he did not belong here. Ever since his promotion and invitation to become a resident of the tower, he felt out of place. He was a soldier, for God's sake, not a socialite. Yet, here he was, attending his first tower function at the request of a certain upper level young lady he'd met in the lounge the night before.

As he listened to the ridiculous story, a fake smile plastered on his face, he was sure the twenty-fifth floor host had no idea who he was. In fact, had he not shown up with Desiree, he was sure the man would've called security.

Evan had only been a resident for a week. His legendary forays into the wilds to secure items of necessity, such as food, water, and medical supplies for the survival of the island dwellers, along with his promotion to captain and his growing financial status had all worked for his nomination and acceptance into the tower. The board of directors overseeing the exclusive island community had voted him in, although it had been a close vote.

The only way for anyone to even be considered for residency was for a board member to sponsor them. Evan had no interest in living in the tower. He preferred to live in the military dorms with his troops, but his commanding officer, General Waters, who lived on the twenty-first floor, had put his name up and talked him into accepting the invitation. He'd regretted it ever since.

Well, at least until he'd met Desiree. Now, twenty-two flights above his own room, he sat with the elite of the island, drinking booze and eating food he couldn't otherwise afford. He thought it ironic that after all the times he'd ventured into the wilds, risking his life and those of his men, he was now getting to enjoy some of the food and drink he'd secured.

The host finished his story and burst into laughter. Evan gave what he hoped was an appropriate laugh and the host slapped his shoulder and moved on to enthrall the next guest. A slim, warm hand slid up his knee and squeezed his thigh. "So, what do you think, Evan?" Desiree's face was aglow, but Evan wasn't sure whether it was because of the party, the booze, or him. He returned her smile, although he didn't think he was able to match the twinkle in her eyes. "It's really amazing."

"It really is. And you should check out the view. Even though it's dark, you can see for a long way up here." Her hand rubbed his leg. It should have been erotic, but instead, her touched annoyed him. "I'll be back in a moment. I have to use the little girl's room." She giggled like a little girl. He supposed compared to him, she probably was. She was barely in her twenties. He was thirty-one.

He watched her go, appreciative of the view. He scanned the spacious room, amazed at how much larger it was his own modest space. His room was much larger than what he shared with the other officers in the barracks, but this area could house at least a dozen troops. The rooms at the lower levels had a front room/ kitchen combination, a bedroom, and bathroom. This apartment had three bedrooms, two bathrooms, a living room and dining room, and a large kitchen. Enough space for the nearly eighty people to move around in.

His gaze became obstructed. He glanced up to see an attractive older woman gazing down at him with a somewhat mischievous smile. "So, you're the new addition to the tower, eh? I must admit, their standards have gone up." She extended a hand. "I'm Felicity Freedman. I live on the floor above."

Evan knew what that meant. She was an elite of the elite. There were only four rooms on the twenty-sixth floor, all belonging to the leaders of the community. Flushed with embarrassment, he stood and accepted her hand. "Uh, I'm Cap, er, I'm Evan."

"I know who you are, Captain. I voted for your admittance." She leaned in close and whispered in his ear. "You owe me." She squeezed his hand, released her grip and dragged a nail provocatively across his palm as she let go. "Hopefully one day soon, you can repay me." She held his eye, sending a flush across his face. He flinched. "Was that a blush? How cute." She turned to move on and said, "You'll see me again." She winked and was gone.

A moment later, Desiree returned. She did not appear to be happy. "So, what did Felicity the Lush want?" She sat down with a huff.

Evan closed his eyes and rolled them behind the lids. He sat down. "She was just introducing herself."

"Yeah. I'll bet." She picked up her drink and finished it.

"Hey, what's the matter?"

"That all depends on whether or not you're going to become another one of her conquests."

A surge of anger touched his response. "I'm no one's conquest." He hoped he conveyed that his statement included her.

She eyed him. "We'll see. I'm going to get another drink." She stood and strode away, never asking if he'd like another. He sighed. *What the hell was he doing here?* His thoughts drifted to Teke, Corporal Tequila Lopez, a member of his team. She was still angry about him accepting the room in the tower. He smiled for the first time all night with any sincerity, thinking of the dark-haired beauty. He knew she liked him. Hell, he liked her, too, but rank and policy prevented anything more from coming of that interest. Still, he hated the fact that she was upset with him. Even if they were unable to develop anything more than a working relationship between them, her respect and friendship were important to him.

For perhaps the millionth time, he thought about what a mistake this had been. He stood and gravitated toward the balcony. For the moment, too many people stood out there for him to join them. He studied the balcony and worried about the safety of that many people on the small ten-foot by eight-foot platform, suspended twenty-five stories above ground. He shook the thought from his mind. It wasn't his job to worry about these people. It was enough that he scrounged for them.

He turned. His gaze swept the room, stopping on Felicity. She was watching him like a tiger on the prowl for fresh game. She puckered her lips at him, then ran a provocative tongue around them. Yep, he was prey. He sighed again and broke eye contact. He moved toward the food table where a wide assortment of appetizers was displayed. He shook his head at the sight. Only the rich would use up this much hard-to-find food for a party. They had no concept of how little food existed out in the real world or what the common folk living elsewhere on the island would give to have any portion of this spread. What a waste. They had no idea how risky it was or how long it took for him and his team to find these rare items. Again, irony struck him. It was because he was so good at it that he had been promoted, resulting in his invitation and acceptance into the exclusive tower.

Oh well; he might as well indulge. He took a small plate, surprised to see it was porcelain and not paper, then reached for a variety of hot and cold foods. He stepped aside and stood by himself, munching. As he chewed, he scanned the room, avoiding the area where Felicity stood. What would be the fallout if he gave up his room and moved back in with his troops? He was sure he could still get his old room back in the officer's barracks. If not, so what? He'd started with the ranks; no reason he couldn't go back there. If they'd have him. He was sure he'd take some shit from them, but what the hell; he could deal with that.

What about General Waters, though? He'd be pissed, and no doubt would take it out on him. Man, what had he gotten himself into? He noticed Desiree standing with a group of friends. Several of them looked his way. They turned their heads away in a hurry when they saw he was watching. Obviously, they were talking about him. This was stupid. He decided to leave. Finishing the food he'd selected, he set the plate down and started for the bar. Just because he was going, no reason he couldn't take a beer with him.

On his way across the room, General Waters' broad body blocked his path. "Give it a chance, son."

"Excuse me, sir?"

"Don't bullshit me, Captain. I know you better than you know yourself. I've been watching you. You feel out of your element; I understand that. It was the same for me when I first got here, but trust me, it gets better. Once you get established, you'll enjoy it. Believe me. It took a while for me, too." He sipped a beer.

"If that cute little girl doesn't work out, there'll be others. Don't let her get you down. I didn't sponsor you here only for the women."

"Why did you, sir?"

Waters smiled. "Because I see great things in you. Your days of exploring and scrounging are fast coming to an end."

"But that's what I'm good at, sir. It's what—it's all I know."

"Right now, maybe, but you can serve a greater good here. Why do you think I've surrounded myself with these people?"

"I really don't know, sir." Evan didn't mean for his reply to come out so judgmental.

Again Waters smiled. "It's because this is where I can do the most good for the troops. Here, I have connections and the ears of the decision makers. Here, I can work for the benefit of the regiment. Why do you think the rank and file got a boost in rations?" He didn't wait for a response. "It was because of my negotiating and working on their behalf. That's what I need from you. I need your help. The more of the military wing we can get inside where the power is and the decisions are made, the better we can look after the troops we command.

"This," he swept an arm out, "may not be our world, but we have to live in it. If we don't have anyone fighting for us, we'll get nothing. You understand? I need you here to help me fight for the troops."

Evan sighed. He understood. Not so much Waters' plans, but the fact he wasn't going to be able to go back to the barracks. "How do you do it, sir? These people have no idea what the real world is like."

"I agree. They isolate themselves in this tower, placing themselves literally and figuratively above the general population. It creates a rift that, in these days and this time in our history, should not exist. But it does. We have to live with it until we can create something different. Something better, where everyone is equal and all do their fair share for the good of the community. We were there initially after the event, but now, after a period of feeling secure, we've fallen back to our old ways of having an elite ruling faction with a feeling of superiority over the rest of us. That's what I'm fighting against. I hope that helps with whatever decision you make."

He finished his beer. "I think I'll get another. Good luck, Captain."

Damn! Was all Evan could think.

3

Corporal Tequila Lopez sat at her post at the bridge gate. Instead of looking outward, though, her gaze held steady and angled upward at the tallest building on the island. The tower, as it was called, was for the elite of the community. Evidently, her captain and secret crush, Evan Stewart, or Stu, as the platoon called him, was now considered an elite. The thought still angered her.

How could he desert them like this? And for what? To be high society? To chase rich poon? That thought angered her more, but why should she care? Couldn't the dumb ass see he didn't belong there? Those snobs would eat him alive. God, he made her so mad. Just another man following the lead of his dick.

Teke scanned the top floors. He had said he was going to a party tonight. Well, la-de-da and good for him. Bastard! She counted the rooms, trying to discern where the party was. What floor did he say it was on? Oh yeah. Twenty-five. She looked at the third floor first to see if his light was on. She knew where it was. She had grudgingly helped him move in. She'd learned a lot about the building since then.

Floors three through fifteen had twenty rooms per floor, ten on each side. From sixteen through twenty, there were sixteen rooms per floor. Twenty-one through twenty-three had twelve per floor. Twenty-four had eight; twenty-five, six; and the top floor, twenty-six, had four very large suites. The higher up the room, the higher your social status. Once in, you worked hard to stay and rise. Secure favor with the higher-ups, and you would rise in position and accommodations. Fall in disfavor, you could drop or be evicted. It was the ultimate in social ladder climbing. Just like before the event.

Teke wondered how long it would take for Stu to get

evicted. She felt guilty for wondering, but she hoped it would be soon. Was she concerned or jealous?

"Man, there sure are a lot of them out there tonight," Private Norton said.

His voice broke her from her thoughts. "Huh?"

"The crits," he said. "There's more out there than I've seen in a long time."

Teke looked as if noticing for the first time. *Damn! There were a lot.* Should she call it in? No, she decided. They were just standing there, which was strange in itself. She wasn't about to raise the alarm and be ridiculed.

"They're really acting weird tonight," Private Morrison said. "They're just standing there, not making any effort at trying to get through the gate. Hell, they're not even touching it."

"Yeah," said Private Manning, a petite brunette. "Usually they're all over the fence. I've never seen anything like it."

"Gives me the creeps," Norton said.

"Everything gives you the creeps," Manning teased.

Movement drew their attention. Sergeant Flanders walked over and stood next to where Teke was sitting. "Something's up, Teke. It's like they're all in a trance. The numbers keep swelling, but none of them have moved toward the gate."

"It's weird for sure," she said, standing. She placed a foot on the cement barricade. "It's almost like they're organized; like they each know what the others are thinking or something."

"Yeah, like they're waiting."

"Yeah, but waiting for what?"

Flanders frowned and shrugged.

"What if they're waiting for a signal?" Norton said.

"A signal? Don't be stupid, Norton. They can't think. They're mindless undead. You're all giving them too much credit."

Teke snorted a laugh. "Could be, but ... there's something." A chill made the hairs on the back of her neck spring to life. She shuddered to shake it off. She swept her gaze along the shoreline, but the darkness was too complete to see far. They only kept one bulb lit out beyond the fence and one inside the gate at the beginning of the bridge. Light and noise drew the crits, so they tried to limit both. If the numbers got too large near the gate, they had standing orders to thin the crowd. But in this instance, none of them were within ten feet of the gate. What did that mean? Was it possible for the creatures to learn? Did they know that getting too close would get them shot?

No. That wasn't possible. The event that had mysteriously brought them back to life was almost three years ago now. In all that time, she had never seen any evidence of anything more than primal hunger in these animals. Feeding was all they knew. Still, this felt wrong.

Over time, the names used to label the animals, and that's what they really were, had changed. In the beginning, they were referred to in the usual ways: zombies, undead, living dead, walkers and many other names. But they were more animal than human in their behaviors, so people began referring to them as creatures or beasts. As was the norm in military ranks, creature morphed to critter, eventually shortening to crit, the common reference now.

Checking her watch, Teke discovered she still had three hours to go before being relieved. Man, she was going to be glad to be off the bridge tonight. It would take quite a few beers to wash this scene from her mind. She looked back at the tower, her gaze stopping on a well-lit room on the twenty-fifth floor. She saw one of the balconies full of people. She wondered if Stu was one of them.

The anger rekindled. Yeah, she was going to have quite a few beers tonight.

"How many do you think are out there?" she asked Flanders.

"Hell, I'd guess several hundred."

Norton snorted. "Yeah, of what we can see."

That froze Teke. She looked at Flanders, who evidently had the same thought and was looking at her. He tugged the radio from his belt and called to the watchtower station at the top of the bridge. "Hey, Jacobson, light up the roadway in front of the bridge."

"You got it, Sarge."

The switch for the large floodlight above was audible. The path beyond the fence looked like it'd been hit by daylight. It took several seconds for their eyes to adjust, but when they did, they both wished they hadn't seen it.

"My God!" Teke said.

"Sweet Jesus," Flanders added.

Stretched in front of them farther than they could see were not hundreds, but thousands of crits, most now agitated by the sudden explosion of light. They became more animated, yet still did not move toward the gate.

"Call it in," Flanders ordered her.

She pulled her radio free, but the clip caught on her belt loop and fell to the cement. She turned and bent to pick it up. As she was rising, movement behind her drew her attention. For a brief moment, she was incredulous at what she was seeing and unable to comprehend it. Then she cried out, "Behind us! Fuck! They're behind us."

Flanders turned, saw the dozens of crits, and said," How the ..." then, "Engage! Engage!"

"You heard the man," Teke said. "Light 'em up."

"Norton, Manning, and Jacobson, direct your fire toward the rear," Flanders commanded. He started to make a call, but one of the men at the front of the defenses yelled. "Hey, they're moving out front."

Flanders and Teke turned to look. "Maybe you were right, Teke. They were waiting for a signal."

"Is that possible?"

"Let's clear the bridge before we get cut off. We can discuss it later."

She lifted her carbine, took aim and fired. The closest crit pitched backward. All along the defensive position, guns blazed while Flanders called in the alert.

4

Unaware of the battle that waged below, Evan finally found room on the balcony and squeezed on. The air was cooler this high up. He closed his eyes and let the breeze refresh him. Someone tapped his shoulder and he turned. It was Felicity.

"Enjoying the view?"

"Yeah. It's not something I see very often."

"That's what I was thinking, too, while I was enjoying the view I had." Her eyes roamed his body from head to toe and back up. Her smile was wicked.

The heat rose to his cheeks again. He hoped in the dark it wouldn't be as evident. She stepped closer and placed her full lips next to his ear. "What do you say the two of us go upstairs to my place and look at the view from a higher and far less crowded vantage point?"

"Ah, I don't know."

"If you're shy, we can keep the lights off." Her hand snaked around his body and grabbed his buttock. She squeezed. "Ooh! Firm. Is everything that hard?" She brushed her lips against his ear, sending a chill down his spine. He couldn't help but lean his head toward her to block any more nibbles.

"I think it'll be much safer right here."

She put on a pout. "Oh, but not nearly as much fun."

She made him feel just as uncomfortable as he would have felt with a crit roaming around him. In fact, that's what she reminded him of. A living crit. She wanted to devour him, too. Just in a slightly different way.

Finding more space near the railing, Evan backed toward it, hoping the move would be a sufficient enough message that he wasn't interested, but Felicity persisted. As he turned to look out, her arm went around his waist.

Her fingers rode up and down his stomach with a practiced, gentle touch. He sighed, wondering how much trouble he'd get in if Felicity accidentally fell over the rail.

Quick flashes below caught his attention. He leaned forward, trying to focus his attention on the bridge. They must be thinning the crits at the gate. He noted a lot of gunshots. Must be an unusual number out there today. He thought about Teke. Was she down there? He was pretty sure she had duty tonight.

"Captain Stewart," General Waters called.

Evan turned. "Yes, sir?"

"Just wanted to say good night."

Thankful for the reprieve from Felicity's wandering hands and an excuse to leave the balcony, Evan walked toward his superior. He drew closer, and noting the man's outstretched hand, grasped it. The general squeezed and pulled, guiding him off the balcony. "Son, I know you're new to all this," he swept an arm, "and to the ways of the rich and spoiled, but just a warning. Be careful who you decide to get involved with. Some of these people play the game much better than you ever could. I wouldn't want you to get evicted so soon after landing here because you took up with another man's wife, especially a man as powerful as Arthur Freedman."

"Ah…yes sir, but I have no intention ..."

Waters held up a hand. "I didn't think you would, but thought it wise to have a word, if only to get you away from her. Just a suggestion, but if you're not going to hook up with the young lady you came with, it might be a good idea to make it an early night. The crowd's starting to thin out now, anyway." He gave a fatherly smile. "Just a thought."

"And a good one, sir. Thank you."

The larger man patted his shoulder. "Good luck, whatever you decide." He turned and walked toward the door. Evan watched for a moment, but then became aware of something nagging at the back of his mind, like a memory stuck there, struggling to surface. He worked at it for a moment, then gave up as Desiree came closer.

She stopped in front of him and gave a shy smile. She looked away, then focused on something over his shoulder. What or whoever she saw there put a sour look on her pretty face. Evan could guess who it was. An instant later, something touched his butt. He tried not to react. Felicity brushed past, giving a sly, yet challenging smile to Desiree. She continued on, turning when she was beyond them, and blowing a kiss at him.

"So, are you going up to her place?" Desiree asked.

"No. I have no intention of doing that."

Desiree's look said she didn't believe him. Again he had the thought he didn't belong in this insanity. His place was down on the bridge with the troops. That thought triggered a memory. Again, an agonizing thought fought to burst through a fog, but clarity remained beyond his grasp.

"Are you sure? Felicity isn't used to people telling her no."

"She's not who I came here with."

That seemed to ease the tension. Desiree smiled and took his hand. "I'm glad your interest is turned in my direction." She moved closer, desire lighting her eyes, her moist lips parting.

He matched her smile and moved to meet her lips. Then the memory surfaced, sparked by her words *turned in my direction*. He stopped, eyes widening as understanding dawned. "My God!" Some of the gunshots had been directed inward, not just outward.

Desiree clearly didn't know what was wrong. "I'm sorry," he said. "I have to check something." He left her, cutting through the crowd in a hurry. He pushed to the front of the balcony and stared down. No muzzle flashes were evident. He began to relax, then realized the lights over the bridge and the fence were out. It was strange for both to be out at the same time.

More flashes appeared. They seemed to be aimed in all different directions. Something was wrong. He reached for the radio that was always on his hip, but it wasn't there.

Momentary confusion cleared as he remembered Desiree had insisted he leave it behind. She had reminded him that he was off duty and it wasn't likely he would need to call for help upstairs. He glanced behind him at where Desiree stood, still confused by his sudden retreat. Curiosity directed his attention downward once more when the alarm went off and the screams from the streets drifted upward.

5

No one at the party seemed to hear anything or be aware of the danger. He took a quick head count. About fifty people remained, most in various stages of inebriation. Desiree came forward, a scowl on her face. She crossed her arms over her chest, struck an attitude pose, and said, "What the hell, Evan?"

He had no time for her childish nonsense. Rather than explain the situation more than once, he cleared his throat and said, "Excuse me. Hey." Only a few people looked in his direction, and then only for a few curious seconds.

"Evan, what's going on?"

He scanned the room for General Waters, but the man was nowhere to be seen. He must have already left. He tried again. "Hey, everyone, listen." The voices and the music combined to drown him out. Frustration and concern mounting, Evan moved with haste to the sound system and yanked the cord. As the decibel level decreased and all eyes turned his way, he raised his voice and shouted. "I need you to listen!"

"Fuck you," one man said. "Put the music back on." He moved to do just that.

Evan grabbed his arm. The man pulled free and spun aggressively on Evan. He had no time for fools. With one quick, short punch, he felled the man to the astonished gasps of the watchers. "Now, you drunken idiots, you need to listen." The room quieted.

He was about to explain when Felicity stepped from the crowd. "What is the meaning of this?" She looked at the unconscious man. "This is why we should never allow your kind into the tower. I want you out of here now, or I will call security."

"I don't care what you want. If you'd quiet down enough,

you'd be able to hear the siren blaring. The island has been breached. Crits are inside the defenses."

Evan's announcement started panicked chatter. His tone less condemning now, the host said, "You're sure of this?"

"Go look for yourself." He pointed toward the balcony. A group hustled in that direction. A wild mass exodus began as Evan's words were confirmed.

"My God!" the host said. "This isn't possible. Shouldn't you be out there doing something to protect us?"

"Yes, I'm going, but I wanted to make sure everyone was aware of what was going on. I'm not sure what the situation is on the ground. You may not be able to get down from here, but you should get armed and stay in groups. Perhaps get to a safe place and lock yourselves in."

"Screw that," one man said. "I've got a family. I need to get them out of here."

"How do you plan to do that with the street crawling with crits?" Evan said.

"You're going to protect us."

"I don't think so. I'm not your personal bodyguard. It's everyone or no one."

The man stepped forward and whispered, "Get my family out of here and I can make it worth your while."

The man's bribery efforts disgusted Evan. Others heard or figured out what was being said and began complaining or negotiating for his services, offering a wide range of options. Their voices rose in anger and desperation until Evan could no longer stand hearing them.

"Shut up!" he shouted. "Shut up and stop thinking only about yourselves. We are all in this together. You decide what you want to do. I've already told you what you should do. I can't help any of you if you all go off and try to get to the ground floor from different directions. The smart thing to do is go in groups and lock yourselves in your rooms until the defense corps can rid the island of the invaders. Whatever you decide, do it now. I have to go down to my room and get my weapons. When I return, I'll hopefully have a better idea of the situation."

That started the debate anew. Everyone spoke at once. Evan fought his way toward the front door, shaking off a multitude of hands grabbing at him and ignoring all the comments, pleas, and offers thrown at him.

Reaching the door, he looked back and noticed Desiree standing ten feet away, looking at him. Huge tears rolled down her face. She looked so defenseless, like a child who'd been separated from her mother. His heart melted, but he didn't have time to babysit her. He opened the door, stopped and went back to her. Embracing her while she sobbed, he whispered, "You wait here. You're safe here. I'll be back in a few minutes." He tried to release her, but she clung tighter. "I'm so scared. Please, don't leave me."

"Desiree, listen to me. I have to go. I need to get my weapons and find out how serious the breach is. You need to stay here until I come back for you. Understand?"

She cried harder. He pulled her arms away, giving her a reassuring squeeze that he knew did anything but reassure, and went back to the door. The way was blocked by people all trying to get out at the same time. Evan hated the self-centered actions of these spoiled, supposed elite. He waded through the middle, yanking, pulling, and shoving to get to the front. There, he turned and faced the crowd. "Work together, or you'll all be stuck here forever. As much as it might be hard for you to do so, help each other. This is no time to panic and turn against one another."

He pointed at a large black man standing near the front. "You, direct traffic here so everyone who wants to leave can get out without getting hurt." With that, Evan turned and exited. In the hall, he debated between the elevator and the stairs. Pros and cons both ways. He opted for the elevator and pushed the call button. The wait was long. Four elevators ran to the twentieth floor, but only two went all the way to the top.

Thinking his choice was a mistake and about to head for the stairs, he heard the *ding* announcing the car's arrival. By then, others had joined him. As the doors slid open, the crowd surged forward. Evan found himself pressed against the door.

Screams burst from those in the front and a violent pushback created havoc. People tried to flee but were either trapped or bounced off each other. Some tripped. Those at the back, not knowing what was going on, only saw open doors and no one moving forward. They began pushing. The screams increased until someone shrieked, "Crits!"

The crowd dispersed in a hurry.

Evan waded forward. Inside the car, two crits were bent over a woman, tearing her flesh away with unclean fingers. The nails ripped and tore. Rotted and blood-soaked teeth gnawed at her bones. A third stood and ambled after the fleeing group of partygoers.

Evan reached into his back pocket and pulled out a folding knife, the one weapon he'd brought with him without Desiree knowing. As the tall crit exited the elevator car, snagging its long fingers into the hair of a plump woman, Evan stepped forward and plunged the blade through the creature's eye. It exploded with a pop. Evan drove the six-inch blade as deep as possible, knowing from vast experience he had to do significant damage to the brain to kill the crit.

He rode the dead thing back into the elevator and withdrew the knife. The crit fell to the floor as the doors slid closed, trapping Evan inside with the other two.

6

Reaching behind him, Evan punched the button for floor three just as one of the crits, a dead woman with much of her decomposed face hanging in thin strips, took a swipe at him. She hit his leg but he danced away. The short monster dining with her pushed to his feet and closed in on Evan. His mouth was circled in blood, making him look like a drunken clown with garishly applied red makeup.

He lifted a foot to kick the beast back, but hesitated, seeing the brown dress shoe. He normally wore combat boots when fighting crits. Most people feared the bite, not realizing that a scratch from those diseased nails was just as dangerous and as deadly. He had no choice. He'd just have to be careful.

Evan drew his leg back and shot a side kick into the thing's chest, propelling him backward into the wall. While he had a moment, he turned his attention to the woman crit who had gone back to tearing into her victim's flesh. He grabbed her filthy hair, much of which tore free from the scalp, and pulled her head back. She snarled and reached for his arm.

There were only a few spots to be sure of a quick kill using a knife. He couldn't risk trying to jam the blade through the skull, having it deflect, or worse, snap. He plunged the honed edge deep into the eye socket.

As he maneuvered the blade back and forth to ensure a kill, the other crit came at him again. Evan drew his leg up and bent his knee. This time, as he snapped the kick forward, the crit managed to wrap his hands around Evan's calf. For an instant, panic bloomed. After all he'd done, everything he'd been through, to die like this was beyond belief, so much so he refused to accept it and regained his normal cold, efficient control.

Yanking the blade free, a portion of the eye still dangling

from the blade, Evan reversed his grip as the animal edged closer, pulling on his leg. Just as the crit bent to take a bite, Evan fired his arm forward, driving the blade through the ear. At the same time, he ripped his leg downward and out of the crit's grasp. From there, trying to stay clear of the flailing hands, he grabbed what remained of its left bicep and pushed, pinning the creature to the wall. Using all his weight and strength, he shoved the blade point deeper, until the body dropped.

The bell *dinged*, announcing his arrival on the third floor. He yanked the blade loose and turned to face whatever might come through the door. His mouth gaped at the chaos and carnage around him. *How had they gotten up here so fast?*

The hall was filled with crits, more than he'd seen in one place since the very beginning of the event. So far, he'd gone unnoticed. Someone screamed. He poked his head out and looked to the left. A woman was trapped under half a dozen crits. As much as he wanted to help her, he realized it was already too late. Her shrieks continued for long moments, sending a chill of sorrow and guilt spiking through him.

He glanced right. His room was at the end of the hall. He had to get through perhaps twenty of the undead to get there. He looked at his bare arms and the efficient, yet small knife. The idea of reaching his room unscathed was absurd. He stepped back. No way. He'd die, even if he did reach the room. One of those foul creatures would surely scratch his exposed arms. Death wouldn't come quick; maybe not for two or three days, but it would come. No, he couldn't allow that. He'd eat a bullet before he allowed himself to become one of them.

The woman's screams ceased. She was gone. A small group of crits went past the elevator door, still unaware of his presence. Evan kept a hand over the door, preventing it from closing. He took another quick peek. With the group that had just passed out of the way, there were fewer crits to get through. He sighed. The gauntlet run was stupid to consider, but his only hope of surviving and getting back upstairs to help Desiree and the others was to get the weapons from his room.

Drawing in all his courage, he darted from the car with the words *this is stupid* playing repeatedly in his head.

He blasted past four of the creatures before any of them could react. He dodged to the left, ducking, then slid back to the right, but always Evan moved forward. He managed to squeeze past three more. He sidestepped and slid along the right side wall, just avoiding an outstretched hand with nails as long as his knife blade, or at least they appeared so to his anxious mind.

Two rooms to go. Suddenly, his way was blocked. Three of them stood shoulder to shoulder across the hall, as if in formation. Evan was forced to stop. With a quick glance behind, he knew he had to get through them, or he was dead. A slew of crits had turned his way as he blew past them and were now closing in. He was surrounded.

Wanting desperately to avoid their grasps, Evan's mind worked fast, searching for an opening. He found it at the spindly legs of the creature on the left. Without hesitation, Evan ran at the crit and dove between the wall and his right leg. The snap of the bone filled the hall. The body collapsed over the top of him, and Evan landed past the undead blockade, rolled to his feet and took off. He didn't waste time looking back, but tried to do a damage assessment without looking at his body. His brain searched for areas of pain. He found several, but they felt more like the aches and pains of bumps and bruises rather than the burning of scrapes or punctures.

Two more came at him, but they were just beyond his door. He reached into his pocket for his keys and again felt panic constrict his breathing as he came away empty-handed. Patting his pockets back and front in desperation, his mind whirled, trying to remember if he'd brought the keys or left them in his room. An image of himself locking the door came clear. No, he had the keys when he left. So where were they, then?

He glanced back the way he came, and he spotted them lying on the floor. They must have fallen out of his pocket when he dove. Sucking in a quick breath, he ran for them. Two-thirds of the blockade had swung around in his direction, while the crit with the broken leg clawed at the commercial grade carpet to turn around. The keys lay not two feet in front of it.

Evan reached the keys and grasped them, but as he tried to stand, the broken-legged creature managed to stretch far enough to wrap his grimy hand around Evan's wrist. A startled cry escaped his lips. Grabbing the dead hand, careful not to drag a nail across his skin, he peeled each finger back until it snapped. He pulled free just as the other two reached him.

Leading with the blade, he punched the closest one in the face. It sliced through what remained of his nose and slid through the eye. He lifted a foot and kicked the body back. As the knife came free, he swiped it across the throat of the second crit. The head hung forward with no support to hold it in place. Evan jumped backward, evading the outstretched arms, and ran back toward his room. The two beyond the door had now crossed to his side of it.

"Damn!" Two more to beat before he could reach safety. He stopped and looked toward the elevator. Many more heading his way. But where had they all come from? Surely, they hadn't ridden the elevator. There were too many of them up here. Looking past the advancing horde, he spotted the answer. Some fool had propped the far fire door open. As he watched, two more crits staggered through it. He had to get inside.

The oncoming two were staggered just enough that he only had to deal with one at a time. He kicked low, striking the first crit's fleshless kneecap. The bones were driven backward in grotesque fashion. The beast tumbled forward. In constant motion, Evan spun away from the still-reaching arm, and once more punched the blade through the eye of a short, plump female creature. One hand clawed at his shirt, tearing the material. He cringed, and out of fear, used both hands to pitch her against the wall. There, she stumbled over the fallen creature.

His way now clear, Evan stepped in front of the door. *Just get it open. Don't look back.* But he could not follow his own advice. The backwards glance increased his angst and he missed the keyhole twice. "Come on! Relax," he muttered. He sucked in a deep breath, and releasing it slowly, seated the key and unlocked the door. He pushed it open, entered and slammed it shut, engaging the lock.

Leaning against the door, he tried to calm his racing heartbeat. Evan glanced around the Spartan- standard apartment. If it hadn't have come furnished, the room would be bare. He stayed there for several minutes, catching his breath and trying to form a plan before remembering the chaos below. Then, one thought burst to the forefront. *What about Teke? Hadn't she been on duty on the bridge tonight?* He prayed he was wrong. Racing to the balcony, he pulled the sliding door open and stepped outside. Though night, he could observe the scene more easily with the building lights and his lower vantage point.

Distant screams filtered up to him. The island had clearly been overrun. How it happened didn't matter for the moment. That could be analyzed and dealt with later. First, they had to survive. He noticed something else, or more accurately, noticed the *absence* of something else, which was very disconcerting. The lack of gunfire meant much of the defense and resistance had failed. Where were the troops? Countless other people had weapons as well. Had they felt safe for so long, they'd gotten out of the habit of having their guns ready?

The island held more than ten thousand people. Surely they could rally and push back the invaders. Where was the organized resistance? Where were the community's leaders? A body fell past him from a balcony somewhere above. He jumped back, startled, his hand automatically reaching for the weapon that was usually a part of his wardrobe. The gun had been his constant companion for how long now, and of course, the one time he really needed it, he'd left it behind to impress a woman. What a fool.

He pictured Teke, her short black hair framing her light brown complexion. Those liquid dark eyes, the slightly crooked, bright smile. She had to be all right. He went back inside and crossed to his bedroom. It was time to get outfitted and save some lives.

7

"Watch behind you!" Teke shouted and squeezed off a round, blowing the back of a crit's head off and saving Norton.

The fighting was intense. With only the six of them on the line and one in the tower, they lacked the firepower to deal with this many crits. They'd become too self-assured. With so little action over the past few months, the number of defenders had been decreased from twenty to its current complement. Teke hoped the oversight wouldn't cost all of them their lives. Still, as long as the gate held and reinforcements arrived, they should be able to wipe out the crits that had somehow gained access to the island and come in from behind them.

The gate rattled.

"Hey!" shouted Morrison. "They're trying to break through the gate."

"You and Wells keep them back while we deal with these," Flanders ordered. He turned to join Teke.

Jacobson's machine gun chattered a deafening cadence, tearing into those pressed against the front of the fence. Though the bullets tore through the undead army, only a few were felled. The rounds were not striking their heads.

"Where's our damned reinforcements?" yelled Morrison over the cacophony of gunfire.

"Don't worry about them. Keep shooting," Flanders responded. "And stop firing full automatic. Make your shots count."

Two of the crits, although hit multiple times, closed in on Norton. The frightened man backed away, firing widely into the bodies. They kept coming.

"The head, you fool!" Flanders shouted. "Aim for the head."

But the panicked man was beyond hearing or rational thought. Screaming, he depressed the trigger on his rifle until his magazine went dry. Still, he kept firing. He ran into the front cement barrier and fell over it backwards. Out of the line of sight now, Teke took aim and fired. The lead crit went down. Flanders targeted the second from behind and fired at close range. The body toppled over the barricade, landing on Norton. He screamed, jumped to his feet and ran blindly, directly in the path of Jacobson's .50 caliber rounds. His body danced as the bullets pierced him. Though Jacobson responded immediately by moving the smoking barrel, the speed at which the machine gun spit was more than enough to riddle Norton with holes, any one being the cause of his death.

Jacobson was not quick enough to see where his rounds hit next. Shocked by the death of Norton, he failed to notice as the large caliber bullets tore through the locks holding the gate. They squealed open, allowing the army of undead entry to the bridge and ultimately to the city beyond.

Morrison yelled, "They're in! They're through the gate."

Both he and Wells fired until their magazines were empty, then hopped the first barrier.

Both Teke and Flanders turned to look. They had made significant headway at clearing away the crits behind them, but they didn't have enough firepower to stop the horde in front of them.

"Call it in," Flanders said as he turned to engage the front line.

Even as Teke placed the call, the reinforcements from the first alert began arriving. They took up positions wherever they could and laid into the crits. The original group who'd come up behind them were finally dispatched, but the numbers crossing onto the bridge were more than any of them had enough bullets to stop.

Morrison managed to hop over the second barrier, but Wells wasn't as lucky. With one foot over, he was yanked backward and his screams and body disappeared under the writhing mass of undead bodies.

"Fuck!" Manning said. "They got Wells. Wells is gone."

"Keep firing!" Flanders commanded.

"I'm out," said Morrison.

"Get to the back and grab more ammo."

Manning followed. "I'm out, too."

"Go," Flanders told her.

Teke and Flanders were much more controlled with their rate of fire. They were slower, but exceedingly more accurate. One after another, bodies dropped in front of them, yet still the massive wall of rotted flesh and bone advanced.

The sudden stoppage of the machine gun was as deafening as the chatter it made while firing.

"Retreat," Flanders said, but it was only himself and Teke. Jacobson descended the long ladder from his perch. Teke stepped behind the last barrier and covered Flanders. He joined her and didn't stop there. The advance was more than they could hold. They continued backing away at a steady pace. More and more men arrived on the bridge. Then, way too late as far as Teke was concerned, the island's alarm system began wailing.

She and Flanders reached the front line of the defenders. More than a hundred men poured fire into the horde. They could not miss, but although many crits dropped, the moving wall continued on. They'd reached the halfway point of the bridge. Teke knew they had to keep the masses contained. Once beyond, the crits would be able to scatter in all directions and the troops would not be able to prevent them from entering the city.

With more determination, as if each man finally realized the potential for destruction, the rate of fire increased. Body after body fell. The crits behind stepped on an ever-growing pile of broken bodies. Bones and chunks of rotted flesh littered the bridge. Still, the crits gained ground at a frightening pace. The defenders were forced to retreat to the last quarter of the bridge.

Teke turned to Flanders. "I'm out. We need to bring up

some buses or motorhomes and block the way."

He nodded. "Go. Grab some men and get them up here." She started to go, but Flanders snagged her arm. "Do it fast, Teke. I'm going to order them to hold here."

She nodded. He didn't have to say what that meant. They would stand and fight until their deaths to keep the crits from entering the city. Fueled by the thought, Teke ran as hard as she could.

On her way, she pulled three men with her. After explaining what she needed, they broke into a run, heading for the row of buses parked along the fence that surrounded island. When they arrived, she discovered the doors were all locked. "What the fuck!" she said. "Why are these locked?"

All the large transport vehicles were supposed to be left unlocked and the keys on board for just such an emergency. It was part of the mass evacuation plan. With only one way off the island other than by boat, it was important to have the vehicles that could transport as many people as possible in a moment's notice.

"Try to break in," she ordered. Then she got on the radio. Three calls later, she had the person in charge of mass transport, an arrogant bastard named Willard. "I don't care; we've got an emergency. We need to get in these buses. You get those keys down here now or I'll send someone to get them and they'll leave you bruised. You understand me? People are dying out here and it's your fault."

* * *

In his bedroom, Evan stripped off his party clothes and began donning his patrol outfit. First, neoprene pants, then a heavy, long sleeved shirt. Thick socks came next. The inner layers in place, he donned his camo gear, pants, shirt and boots. Then came the belt, thin gloves, and balaclava. On top of that, he yanked a thick woolen beanie over his ears.

Dressed, his armament came next. His assault rifle was in the barracks, but he had other options here. On his belt, he slid two long bladed knives, one with a serrated edge and one finely honed. He opened and checked the contents of two pouches clipped in place on the belt. One held a first aid kit and survival equipment; the other, four full magazines.

He pulled out two of his three handguns, both 9mm. 9mm ammo was still easy to find, making the it the most popular choice. He pulled them one at a time from their holsters to check the magazines. He chambered a round into each, then placed one holster on his right hip and tucked the other in his belt at the small of his back. He took out six boxes of ammunition and put them in whatever pockets or pouches they would fit. With the six magazines, he had three hundred ninety rounds. From the number of crits in the tower, he hoped it would be enough. Last, he picked up his radio.

"Stewart to base. Stewart to base." He waited. Nothing but static. "Stewart to anyone." More static. Then, a blast of sound. "Captain ..." a crackling stole away the rest of the words from whoever responded.

"Come in. Hello? I need a SITREP."

"Captain." A new voice spoke. Female and familiar.

"Corporal? Is that you?"

"Aye, sir."

His heart skipped a beat, happy to hear her voice and know she was all right. He wanted to ask how she was, to tell her how glad he was to talk to her, but this was neither the time nor place. He swallowed a strange lump and said, "Report."

"The bridge is lost. We have dropped back to the secondary defenses. We're holding so far. I'm going to move buses to block off the flow."

"Good idea. Losses?"

"Significant."

"How did they breach?"

"I don't know, ah, sir. Suddenly, they were behind us. Then, as if orchestrated, a massive horde swamped the gate. There weren't enough of us to hold it and we were forced to retreat. We lost five there."

"I'm, er, I'm glad you're all right."

"Stu--I mean, Captain, the tower is overrun. They're

inside, maybe a thousand strong. There are so many of them between us and the building, we can't get to it."

"I noticed."

"Will-will you be all right?" Her voice held genuine concern.

I hope so. "I'll manage."

"Just stay locked in your room until help arrives."

"Negative, Corporal. Too many people need help here. I have to go. You get control down there, then come for us."

"Yes, sir."

"And Teke, stay safe."

Pause.

"Affirmative, sir."

8

Outfitted and feeling more protected, Evan went to the front door. He listened, but heard nothing. At least there were no screams. That meant either the inhabitants of this floor had found safety behind a locked door, or they were all dead.

Opening the door a crack, he peered out, discovering the hallway was more crowded now than it had been. To the left, the stairwell door stood open, admitting a steady throng of crits. No escape lay in that direction. With dread, Evan realized he would have to fight his way to the right, which meant the entire length of the hall. The only other option would be the elevator, but he wouldn't know the viability of using it until he was already committed to his course of action.

He closed the door. This would take some thought. Even armed and protected, the chances of maneuvering the crowded hall without getting taken down was fifty-fifty. He leaned against the wall and raced through possible scenarios. In the end, the only plan he could come up with that might have a chance to work was to draw the crits to one end and lessen the number of them he would have to fight through.

He closed the sliding door leading to the balcony, but left it unlocked. Back in his bedroom, he opened the window and leaned out. *Can I reach the balcony from here?* He stretched an arm out to get an idea of the distance he would have to jump. He glanced down. Three floors were a long way to fall.

Studying the window, looking for more space and something to hold onto, he began to doubt the sanity of the plan. The pane opened from the top and pulled out at an angle. To make it through, he would have to get above the window and slide down. Once outside, there was a ledge about a three-inches wide to balance on; not much room to stand on, let alone push off of. Only one way to know for sure.

Pulling over a hard-backed wooden chair, Evan stood on it and stepped over and through the window's opening. Finding purchase on the ledge, he tested it with some weight. He would have to hold onto the frame for added support, providing it didn't break away in his hand. Bending his knee, he hoisted his leg up and over, placing his foot next to the other one. He leaned backward into the room. The tricky part here was to lower his body through and still maintain his footing. He did so slowly, realizing he would not have this much time once he set the plan in motion. He would have to be much faster, or falling would be the least of his worries.

Ducking his head under the frame, he now hung outside. The balcony was eight feet away. He stretched, holding onto the window frame with one hand. He was so close, but to reach the metal railing around the balcony, he had to release his grip on the window frame and jump.

He looked down again, spotting a small patch of grass that extended from the building, then nothing but cement. But from this height, would landing on the grass be that much better? He had no choice. He had to try. A lot of people's lives depended on him getting out of his room. The longer he delayed, the more people would die.

Taking a few quick breaths, he counted down and prepared to push. Just before letting go, he stopped. This was crazy. There had to be a better way. *No! Do it! Now!* Sans countdown, Evan let go and pushed off the narrow perch. He stretched as far as his body would go. His eyes widened at the sight of the railing before him, his fingers splayed wide. Then, impact. The balcony came at him so fast, contact almost jarred his hands free from their grip on the spindles.

His feet slipped and his chest smacked into the concrete platform, knocking the wind from him. He hung by his arms, fighting for air. Pain shot through him. *Had he broken a rib?* Pushing the pain aside, knowing he would only be able to hang so long before his considerable strength waned, Evan pulled. Hand over hand, he climbed until he was able to wrap an arm over the top rail. From there, he lifted a leg and managed to get it on the small space outside the railing. The rest was easy. He stepped over the rail and stood breathing hard on the balcony.

"Piece of cake," he said, still gasping.

He had to move before he changed his mind and decided he didn't much like cake.

Opening the sliding door, he stepped inside, closing it behind him. He checked his weapons, walked to the front door, then had a thought and went back to draw the blind on the sliding door. At the front door, he again cracked it open. He held out slim hope that the crits had moved on and his leap would not be necessary. If anything, however, the hall looked more jam-packed than before. Or maybe it was just his imagination, hoping to prevent him from doing what he was about to do.

No turning back. People were counting on him. One deep breath, and he was ready. Flinging the door open, he pulled one of his long-handled combat knives, stepped into the hall and skewered the head of the first crit he saw, a short, old woman. He ripped the blade free, looked down the hall toward the elevator and stuck another creature. The hall was full. They ran into each other like human bumper cars. Well, not quite human.

He turned in time to see arms reaching for him. Ducking, he came up next to the deformed creature and drove the blade through his ear. Unlike his pocket knife, Evan had no fear of driving this blade through any part of the skull. The body dropped as he pulled it free. The crits nearest him began taking notice. Thank God they moved so slow. He backed away and into his apartment. Not wanting to move too fast and lose them, Evan stopped in the front room and waited. The first crits entered ten seconds later.

As more tried to gain admittance to their potential feast, the doorway became impassable. He hadn't thought about that. Feeling like he was telling a joke, he wondered how many crits could fit in an apartment.

As they squeezed through the doorway and the totals grew, he backed farther away. Perhaps twenty of the foul creatures ambled toward him. Evan reached the doorway to his bedroom. He stood there for a moment, then decided he needed to be in position when they came in or he might not have enough time. Running the few steps to the chair, he stepped up and over the frame.

At the faster pace, his foot missed the ledge. He sunk down, smacking his thigh across the frame. He cried out in pain. A scraping sound made him turn his head. They were already in the room and moving toward him.

Don't panic!

The force of his weight shut the window and pinned his leg. The crits came closer. The first one, tall and rail thin, had one eye missing and the lower portion of his jaw gone. Sweat poured in rivulets, as Evan's heart rate spiked. Leaning inward, he pushed off the frame and forced the window back open with his leg.

Trying not to look, but aware his death was mere feet away, Evan planted his foot again. This time, he managed to secure a solid ledge. Standing, he lifted the other leg and lowered it through the window. The move turned him so he now faced the oncoming crits, the first wave not three feet away. He slid his body down in a hurry, scraping his back on the on the latch. Cursing, he ducked under the ledge, banging his head in the process. Fast was no way to make this move, but as the first creatures reached the window, he knew he had no other choice.

On the other side of the window, Evan began breathing easier. All that was left was to make the jump. He made his count, reached two, and was about to launch from the ledge, when an excruciating pain shot through his hand. His foot slipped, and for a moment, he thought he might fall. His first horrified thought was that he had been bit, but when he looked back, he discovered the crits' bodies had pressed against the window, shutting it on his fingers. As more weight was applied, Evan screamed. He was unable to free himself. Then, his worst fear was realized. A crit gripped his fingers and bent to bite him.

"No no no no no!" Evan shouted and tried to extricate his fingers. The gloves he wore were tough, but he doubted they would stand up to much of a grinding by teeth. He grabbed the hilt of the serrated knife on his left hip. Cutting his fingers off was better than being bitten. He hesitated. He felt teeth touch his fingers. He anticipated a crushing pain any second. Reaching for his gun instead, he looked through the glass. The crit attempting to bite him was the one with no jaw.

Evan slid a gun from its holster, lined the barrel even with the crit's head against the pane, and pulled the trigger. The glass shattered and the bullet tore out a chunk of his attacker's face. Pushing the barrel through the broken window, he fired point blank into the heads of the first group. As they fell away, the next row pressed forward, but Evan had a brief respite, just enough time to push the frame inward with his foot and drag his injured right fingers out.

As soon as they were clear, he fell away from the window. Twisting his body, he pushed off the narrow ledge as hard as he could, directing his efforts toward the balcony. Doubting his injured hand's ability to grab and hold, he tossed the gun through the rail so he could use his left hand. It turned out to be a lifesaving move. The fingers of his right hand were useless to hold the rail, but his left did, leaving him dangling by one arm.

He couldn't help but look down three floors below. Maybe he would survive the fall. Then again, maybe not. Death would be better than breaking a leg and being at the mercy of the crits. Pushing all thoughts of falling aside as unacceptable, Evan swung his weight in pendulum fashion until he had enough built-up momentum to secure his right foot between the rail spindles. From there, he wedged his right arm up to the shoulder between two spindles. He gathered his reserves and pulled up and over from there.

Breathing hard, he wiped the sweat from his eyes with his

sleeve and bent to pick up the gun. Looking back at the window, he saw numerous forms leaning out and reaching toward him. *Bastards! I hope the frame breaks and you all fall to the ground.*

He waited a moment to compose himself after his several near-misses with death, taking stock of his equipment. He discovered the serrated knife was gone. All things considered, not that great a loss; it could've been a gun. Evan slid the balcony door open wide enough to look inside. Using the gun barrel, he inched the curtain to the side. His front room was full of undead, but most were trying to get into his bedroom. The front door stood open. Only one crit woman stood in the way. This was his best opportunity.

With care, he opened the door wide enough to step inside, however, he kept the curtain covering him until the last moment. When it would stretch no farther, Evan bolted for the door. Gun leveled, he fired one round as he'd been trained and done many times before: one bullet per crit. Get close, shoot, move on. That was the rule. Of course, it didn't always work, but up close like this, it was much easier to do. The female crit fell back, replaced by a short, heavy black creature.

A second shot resulted in a second body down. The doorway was clear now. Stepping into the hallway, he was forced to shoot twice more before he could shut the door, trapping several dozen crits inside. Less to deal with. He could always come back and take care of them later, providing he was still alive to do so. However, one of the crit's arms was in the way, preventing the door from latching. He tried to move it aside with his foot, but the mass in the hall was coming his way.

He left the door slightly ajar. He just had to get down the hall. Now there were only about two dozen undead between him and there. He sighed. At least he had improved the odds.

9

After glancing left and seeing more crits still coming up the steps, Evan made his way down the hall, gun in one hand, knife in the damaged other. He wanted to save as many bullets as possible. For the most part, that was easy to do. Initially, only a few crits were aware of his presence. He switched the knife to his good hand. Quick jabs dispatched them and he moved on. However, as he closed on the elevators, he drew a bigger crowd and was forced to shoot his way there.

Round after round found a target and dropped a body. In one motion, he holstered one gun and drew the other. Careful of where he stepped, he reached the elevator and through a gun smoke-filled haze, pressed the button. The doors receded at once.

Stepping into the car was dangerous. If he couldn't get the doors closed quick, he risked being trapped. He hit the button for the twenty-sixth floor, then stood waiting to repel advancing crits. He fired once, then the doors finally began to close at an agonizing pace. Two more creatures came to the door. He aimed, but held his fire, thinking they would close before he needed to defend. To his shock, the doors slid back open and the two pushed in. In rapid succession, Evan pulled the trigger. Two shots, two bodies. More were closing in.

He hauled the bodies into the hall and piled them on top of each other, hoping they would serve as a blockade. When he reached the body on the bottom, he discovered why the doors had opened. It had been laying across the threshold. He dragged and tossed it on the pile and reentered the car. This time, the doors closed. With relief, he sagged against the wall as the car began to climb.

He wiped his face again, then looked at the ceiling. He had to get on top of the car in case crits also controlled the floor he was approaching. Stepping on the guard rail, he rose high enough to grip the small pull handle and lower the panel. He gripped the edge and muscled himself up just as the elevator slowed. A *ding* sounded, letting him know he'd arrived, but after sliding along the roof and getting in a position where the car was in view, he noted the elevator had stopped on the fourteenth floor.

The doors opened. As soon as they were wide enough, a woman fell into the car, followed closely by three crits. The woman screamed and kicked violently. Evan hesitated, unsure if she had already been bitten or scratched, but he was unable to remain idle and watch her begin to get torn apart. Whether she died now or later didn't matter. Right now, she was still human. He leaned forward and took four shots to drop the three ghouls.

Surprised at her good fortune, the woman looked around, fear widening her eyes. When she spotted Evan, she relaxed a bit and began to cry.

"Get up and clear the doors."

She sat up, but didn't make a move for the door.

"Hurry," he urged. "Before more of them come."

That got her moving. Using her feet from her sitting position, she kicked and shoved the bodies out of the doorway. She stood, pushed the **close door** button, and looked up at him. The doors started toward each other. She smiled at him. "Thanks, I thought I was--"

Two sets of bony hands reached through the door and yanked her from the car just before the doors touched together.

"No!" he shouted. He jumped down and pushed the **open door** button, but it was too late. Slipping his fingers between the seam, Evan pried with all his might, but the car was already ascending. Her screams filled the shaft and rode with him all the way to the top. Crestfallen at the loss, he almost waited too long to climb back to the roof. This time, the car reached the twenty-sixth floor. He wanted to start at the top and work his way down, clearing the floors as he went.

The car glided to a stop, bounced once and settled. The doors slid open. Muffled shouts came to him first. Still, he waited. Then a curious crit stopped at the elevator and looked in. The doors shut in its face. Fearful someone else might push a button and send the car down to a floor he didn't want to be on, Evan dropped from the roof, changed magazines and leveled his gun. He then pulled his knife and pushed the **open door** button. Again they slid open, and again the crit stood staring. Not sure how many others he had to deal with, Evan lunged forward with the knife.

The crit obliged by moving toward him. Still angry over the lost woman, Evan drove the blade in as far as it would go, then twisted it before pulling back. He used his foot to shove the undead man off his knife. Before the body hit the floor, he was already out of the car. With a quick glance up and down the corridor, seeing he had time, he kicked the body between the elevator doors to keep them open in case he needed a hasty retreat.

To his left, he had six targets. To the right, eight. The fire door on the left was closed; the right one, open. Even though he had more targets that way, he chose right. He needed to close that door. In an advancing combat stance, Evan marched forward. He took the first undead woman with the knife, then rapid fire, one shot per target, he mowed down the remaining seven. He reached the door the same time as a large black crit from the opposite side.

He ducked to avoid the outstretched arms. This creature seemed faster than the others. He went after Evan like a wrestler trying to corner an opponent. Evan ducked and rolled out of the way. From behind his back, he fired three times to drop the beast. As soon as he was sure the crit wasn't going to move, he crawled to the door, lifted the foot latch with his hand and hauled the door shut just as two more crits reached the top step.

He sat trying to catch his breath. The last one had unnerved him a bit, but he could not afford to delay long. The six from the other direction were getting nearer. He stood, dropped the magazine and counted his rounds. Wouldn't do him any good to be in the middle of a fight and run out. He'd used ten of his fifteen bullets. One had to go down with the knife.

Again he moved forward, dispatching crits with deadly efficiency from a distance of two to three feet away. The slide locked back on the last one, but he had expected that. He dodged an arm, stepped to the side, and pounded the blade through the top of the skull. The floor was clear. He changed out magazines.

He knew the next floor might not be as easy and it was also where the party had been. As he went toward the fire door, he wondered how many were still there and still all right. He thought of Desiree. He hoped she was still alive. He did not relish the idea of having to put her down if she'd been turned.

Damn! He hadn't noticed before, but the fire doors on this level did not have a window in them like the lower floors did. He supposed the über-wealthy did not like to be stared at through windows like they were exhibitions at a zoo. Whatever the reason, it meant he would have to go through the door blind. He opened the door a crack, but it didn't help. He had no choice. Inching the door open, he'd gone about eight inches when the door struck someone or something. He started to reverse the path, but a hand with long, gray crusty fingers wrapped around the door. He tugged, but had resistance. Then, the matching hand got a grip, accompanied by a second pair with shorter, thicker fingers.

Well, if he couldn't close it, he'd give them what they wanted. Evan rammed his shoulder into the door, feeling the bite of pain run through his arm and upper back. Digging his feet in, he drove forward until the door swung open with ease.

On the floor were the two that held the door. A quick glance showed six more on the stairs. Without hesitation, he waded through them, making each shot count. In less than two minutes, all eight were down. More were climbing the stairs and stood between him and the fire door. They were on the twenty-fifth floor. In an inane moment, Evan wondered if they got winded at all, climbing that many flights.

He looked over the banister and down the seemingly endless flight of stairs. Crits filled the entire route. Getting out of there was going to be a bitch.

10

"It's about fucking time!" Teke shouted at the man with the keys.

"Hey, I'm sorry. I only did what I was told to do. Who knew we'd get invaded? And before you go yelling at me, wasn't it your job to make sure it didn't happen?"

Fury exploded behind her eyes and she looked at the man through a haze of red. Without thinking, Teke shoved her gun under the man's jaw. "You gotta complaint? Tell it to the complaint department."

"Okay! Okay. I'm sorry."

She released him and he unlocked the door. Snatching the keys from his hands, she tossed a set to one of the other men. "You two grab the bus behind us and follow." They took off at a run. She busted past key man and jumped into the driver's seat. Starting the engine, she revved it and looked around at the dash.

"Ah, I don't mean no offense, so don't shoot me or nothing, but do you know how to drive one of these?"

She looked at him, biting back her initial response. "I've driven the transport trucks, but never a bus. It's got to be about the same, right?"

He frowned, looking toward the bridge, and said, "Get out of there and let me do it. You just keep the crits off me."

"Okay. But we have to hurry."

"What do you want me to do?" the third soldier said.

"Give me a spare magazine." He dug in his utility pack and produced a full mag. He handed it to her. "Keep the crits away until we get going, then jump on the bus behind us."

He slid his rifle from his shoulder and took a defensive stance.

The bus lurched forward, throwing her off balance. Making a hard left to get on the road, the driver swore. The headlights cast long spotlights on the ever-growing number of invaders. They closed the distance in a hurry. The driver began to slow as he got closer to the horde.

"Keep going!" Teke shouted. "Just plow through them. It'll be less of them we have to shoot." Teke felt the dread gather in her chest. If this many crits were already in the city, what had happened to Flanders and the rest of the defense force?

The bus leaped forward, gaining speed, and bounced, hitting and running over crits as they drew closer to the bridge. Teke moved behind the driver and peered hard out the window, trying to find Flanders and the defensive line. The absence of muzzle flashes concerned her.

"Pull up across the bridge as far as you can go. Don't leave any room for them to get around us."

"Okay. I hope the guy behind us knows how to brake."

"Don't worry about him. Just get in position." Silently, she prayed for the same thing.

The driver slowed and guided the bus up the roadway to the bridge, then angled sideways. Teke was astonished and fearful of the moving mass of undead on the bridge. To her great sorrow, she realized any of the soldiers still out there were dead. She prayed Flanders had ordered a retreat before it was too late.

"What's this fool doing?" the driver shouted as a horn blared. Teke snapped her head in the direction where he was looking. At first, she thought whoever was driving the second bus was coming in hot and on a collision course, but it was approaching from the wrong direction. As the distance shortened, she saw the approaching vehicle was a large motorhome, the kind owned by some of the wealthier inhabitants of the island. Someone was trying to make an escape.

Another horn joined the first. There was a loud crash behind them. In its desperate, high-speed flight to escape, the motorhome crashed into the trailing bus. Teke watched as it veered left after the impact, smashing into the bridge abutment. The bus continued forward and out of control, smashing into the rear end of her bus. The jarring impact threw her over the seat and to the floor. The bus began to roll.

"That bastard pushed us over the edge. I'm standing on the brakes, but I don't know if I can hold it. The riverbank is too steep."

Teke got to her feet, then tensed as gunfire erupted close by. With carbine raised, she moved toward the back of the bus, which now was like climbing a hill. The angle was steep, but didn't appear to be getting worse. What she saw when she got there stopped her heart cold.

"You fool!" she shouted, knowing he couldn't hear her. Parker, the rider on the second bus, had opened the door, presumably to get out, but instead had allowed the crits to get in. He swung his gun around, not aiming, rapid-firing from panic. The creatures pressed forward.

The driver, Private Henson, was pinned in his seat, but he tried to shoot around Parker. Teke slid into the last seat and struggled to pull the window down. It broke free at last. By the time she slipped the carbine through the slit, Parker was being hauled off the bus by rotted, decrepit hands tearing at his skin. His terrified screams added to a night already full of death and agony. She lined up a shot, knowing it was already too late for him, but just before she squeezed the trigger, the second bus rocketed forward and rammed her vehicle, throwing her into the next seat.

As the angle of the bus increased, the last thing she saw was Henson being born down. The bus rolled down the embankment toward the water. The driver screamed and jumped for the door. Careening at a dangerous angle, the bus hit the water and tipped on its side. The driver's section quickly filled, but where Teke was hung up remained dry and still on land.

Climbing down, she found the driver floundering in the cold rising water. She snagged an arm and hauled backward, dragging him far enough that he could grip a seat. As an afterthought, she stepped into the water and pulled the ring of keys from the ignition, pocketing them.

"You all right?" she asked.

He coughed and nodded his head.

"We have to get out of here before they descend on us."

"The emergency exit is in the back."

"Okay. Let's try that first and hope we still have time to get out."

Hand over hand, they scaled the seats. When they reached the back, Teke peered out. "Damn!"

"What?" The panic was barely contained.

"Some of them are already starting down after us. We have to get out of here now, or we'll be trapped." The bus slid farther down the bank and deeper into the river, adding motivation for a fast exit.

She grabbed the emergency exit door latch and pulled up. It did not budge. "Shit! Am I doing something wrong?"

"Let me try." She stepped aside, watching the crits' slow but steady approach as he slid past her. After several grunt-filled pulls, he stopped. "The crash must have jammed the door. Help me."

The two of them grabbed hold and pulled with every ounce of strength they possessed. Still, the door would not move.

"Ahhh!" Teke went crazy on the door as an attempt to relieve anxiety. She calmed as fast as she had exploded. "Okay! Okay! We can still do this. Doesn't one of these windows break out?"

"Yes, but," he pointed to the side the bus rested on, "it's on that side."

She glanced at the rising water. That didn't worry her. For the moment, they were too high on the bank for the it to reach them. "Then we have to bust out one of these windows." She raised the butt of her carbine and drove it into the glass. The shatterproof window took multiple hits before it broke from its casing. Teke put a gloved hand through the opening and peeled the glass away. The driver reached up to help and almost immediately cried out. His palm was slashed by the shards.

Agonizing, slow minutes later, the opening was clear. The space was small, but it was their only option. All the other windows were the same size. The driver tried to push his way past her to get out, but Teke put a hand on his chest. "I'll go first. That way, I can cover you."

He started to object, but she cut him off. "In case you hadn't noticed, the noise I made breaking out the window drew more attention. I need to thin the herd if we're gonna get out of here." That settled any dispute. Standing on the side of the seat, Teke muscled her way through the opening to the side of the bus that was currently the top. Swinging her legs out, she stood, pulled the carbine from her shoulder, and began picking off the lead invaders.

To her great annoyance, the driver struggled to lift his bulky frame through the escape hatch. Teke was forced to stop shooting and haul him out. Even then, he was winded and unable to move.

"Look, man, if we don't move now, we may never be able to. I don't care how tired you are. Rest when we're safe."

She forced him to his feet, then without looking back, made for the front section of the bus. It was lower to the ground and farther away from the crits. Advancing to where the bus had entered the water, she leaped off, landing at the shoreline. She hit the hard-packed, damp sand and rolled once, coming up with her weapon ready to fire and aware that the magazine was less than half full.

The grunt and subsequent groans told her the driver had landed. Without looking, she reached a hand down and helped him up. "I think I twisted my knee."

"I can't help you. I'm gonna be busy keeping those animals off us."

"But I can't run."

"Then walk fast. Would you rather have pain in your knee, or pain all over your body from bites? You decide."

He started to hobble.

"Over there," she motioned with the barrel. "Head that

way. I'll cover you."

As he started up the hill, his movement drew the attention of a dozen crits. They turned toward him, their pace only a bit slower than his.

Teke raised the carbine, sighted and fired. Her plan was to shoot the leaders so he could gain some distance and the crits would be drawn to her instead. However, she could only afford a few shots, choosing to save some for more dire situations.

Once the driver reached level ground and ambled off toward the row of shops along the riverfront, Teke began her climb. She slipped once, then tripped over a cluster of rocks before landing on her knee. "Shit!" she muttered. "Now, I'm a gimp, too." Pushing the butt of the carbine into the ground, she levered her body upright and continued her climb. Once at the top, she no longer saw the driver, but now a host of crits was in pursuit of her as well.

Lifting the carbine, she aimed and fired one round. An undead woman pitched forward, but the others turned toward her. That had been her plan, but now that they were closing in on all sides she saw the error of her thinking. She had not left herself an escape route.

11

Evan pulled the second gun. This would take more than a knife and gun. Two guns might not even be enough, but if he was going to do this, he had to do it now before more crits reached the top. Telling himself how crazy it was, he started down.

His weapons barked left and right, leaving a trail of bodies all the way to the first turn. *Halfway there.* Bone fragments filled the air like confetti. One step at a time, he descended, lining up a shot to the right, then to the left. He needed to reach the fire door before both guns emptied. With both hands full, reloading would be slow.

Three steps. Two more shots. Two steps. Two more shots. One step. No more shots. Both guns ran dry. In a flash, he holstered one gun and clubbed a young boy crit out of the way with the other. He pulled the knife, kicked another creature to the side, stuck the knife in still another, and reached for the door handle. He gripped it as several hands grabbed at him.

In a wild flurry, Evan spun, kicking and slashing, while still keeping one hand on the handle. He pulled, but he was in his own way. A quick jab with the knife, a punch with the gun, and a front kick sent a group of crits flying down the stairs, impacting against others and starting a snowball effect. It gave him the room he needed to slip through the door.

Several undead patrolled the hall here, but someone evidently had the foresight to close both doors before they had become inundated. He loaded both guns, pocketed the empty magazines, and made short work of the seven crits on the floor.

After clearing it for the moment, he leaned against the wall to get his breath, dropping the partial mag, and refilled it from one of the boxes. With two full guns now, he went down the hall and knocked on all the doors, proclaiming the floor was safe.

A few cracked their doors a bit to check. Most did not respond, either from fear or because there was no one home. He went to the unit where the party had been and pounded. "The hallway is safe. Come out."

A male voice called from behind the door. "How do we know you're not one of them?"

"Seriously? When was the last time you heard a crit speak? Get your ass out here so we can make some plans." Slowly, one by one, five of the six doors opened and cautious, scared people emerged. The last door on the right remained closed. "Does anyone know if they're home?"

The host, whose name Evan couldn't remember, said, "They were down in the lounge when everything went crazy. I don't know if they made their way back or not."

Evan scanned the group. There were maybe thirty people. "We need to open that door, then. I want everyone here to discuss what we're going to do. I'll need some of you to pull out dressers, buffets, and any other large wooden items we can use for a blockade."

"Excuse me," the host's wife said. She was a short, rotund woman with dyed black hair. "Who do you think you are, giving us orders?"

"I'm the man with the guns who's trying to save your ass."

She huffed and the host raised his hands. "If anyone is going to lead here, it will be me."

Surprised and annoyed, Evan said, "By all means, lead away." He swept his arm in a mocking flourish.

"Ah, I'll need one of your guns."

"Not happening."

"How dare you?" his wife said. "Do you have any idea who you are talking to?"

"Lady, I don't care. I risked my life retrieving these guns so that I could come up here and rescue you. Look at the bodies. I didn't see any when I got here. You'd all be stuck in your rooms until you rotted away and became one of them. I cleared the floor above and this one. That's a start, but we have to move now to keep them clear. The longer you talk, the harder it will be to get out of here. Now, you either start moving furniture, or I'm leaving you to your fate. What's it gonna be?"

Many of them muttered, some complained. Others refused. One man stepped forward His tall, well-built frame was accentuated by his expensive gray suit. "What do you need?"

Evan offered him a smile. "We need large pieces of furniture moved into the stairwells to block any other crits from getting up here. That way, we'll have two floors safe."

Felicity, her tone more frigid than it had been earlier, said, "Why can't you just shoot your way downstairs and bring up more people to rescue us?"

"For one, I don't have enough bullets. For another, most of the defense forces are busy on the streets, propelling the invasion. I was in radio contact with one of my officers. She informs me that they have been overrun. The bridge is lost. She estimates the crits' numbers to be in the thousands. If it were anyone else, I'd think that was an exaggeration. Judging from how many I've already put down, I don't doubt her estimation."

"Can't we just follow you down?" another woman asked.

"I'm sorry, no. Same reason. I don't have enough bullets to keep you all safe, and my attention would be twisted in so many directions worrying about all of you, I wouldn't be able to do a good job. For the moment, we're safer staying here. Let's barricade the floor and decide what to do from there."

While he'd been talking, he noticed two men moving around the outside of the group and coming toward him from opposite directions. Evan hadn't considered them a threat, but then he caught a nod from the host at something over his shoulder and the hairs on the back of his neck rose.

He turned to the left and threw an elbow into the onrushing man's face. His nose erupted in a gout of blood. The man on the opposite side managed to get his hands on him, but Evan brought the gun up and clipped him on the side of the head, dropping him to the floor, shrieking. Meanwhile, the host and another man moved on him. Evan cocked the hammer and pushed it against the host's forehead.

For a long, tenuous moment, no one moved. A few cried out in fear and surprise. "If you are unhappy with my leadership, you are welcome to take over. I'll be leaving. I know I can make it alone."

Desiree stepped out from behind the crowd. She placed a hand on the barrel and pushed it down. "I'm with you. Where do you want to start?"

He smiled at her and lowered the gun.

"Look, I'm not the enemy. I've fought these creatures for several years and I know what I'm doing. My suggestions are for your safety. I'm sorry if that means sacrificing some treasured furniture, but would you rather sacrifice your lives? I need some cooperation and your help."

The tall man in the suit said, "Come on, everyone. He's right." He slid out of his jacket. "I'm Jack. Where do you want us to start?"

"Evan. Let's start with the room closest to the stairs."

Jack turned to the group, looking over them. "Bob and Barbara, that's you. Let's go." He led them away.

"We also need someone at the other end. At no time should anyone open those doors unless I say so. Understood?" He got grudging approvals, but that was better than dissension.

Desiree and four others broke off and headed to the opposite end. The remaining group, including the big shots, stayed put. Evan knew they would be trouble later, but he had no time to deal with them now. If they didn't want his help, he would lead the rest to safety and they could fend for themselves. He couldn't protect those who didn't want to be protected. He followed Desiree's group.

He glanced back to see Jack and his people disappear into an apartment. Evan couldn't watch both teams. He had to hope the other squad would do as instructed. They stopped at the end of the hall and a tall black man unlocked the door. Evan was close behind as he stepped inside. Brushing past the man, Evan inventoried the furniture.

"The two dressers, that buffet out in the dining room, and the sofa. Let's get them out in the hall," Evan said.

The tall black man, Ervin, bent and grabbed the bottom of the dresser. Evan took the opposite side. They shuffle stepped all the way into the hall before putting it down to the side of the fire door with the growing collection of furniture. Barbara's voice thundered down the hall. "I told you, not that piece. That's an antique. It's been in my family for generations."

Jack said, "Tell me, Barbara, who's going to take care of your precious antique after those creatures eat you?"

Barbara sputtered, but no longer made any comment. Evan decided he liked Jack.

Piece by piece, the items he requested were delivered. As the sofa was being manipulated through the door, Evan jogged to the other end. He spoke to Jack, trusting that he would follow directions.

"I'm going out that door." He pointed toward the far end of the hall. "I'll clear it and we'll set the barricade. Then I'll go up and around and come down these stairs. Listen for me. As soon as I signal, open the door and build the barricade here. Do not open the door until I'm ready. Understood?"

"Yeah. We can do this."

Evan flashed a quick smile. He turned toward the far side, then stopped. Pulling out his backup gun, he handed it to Jack. "If something happens to me, keep these people safe."

Jack took the gun and looked at it.

"You do know how to use it, right?"

"Yeah."

"Okay. See you in a few minutes." He trotted toward the others, hoping that was true.

12

"I need one person to go with me." He looked around at the scared faces. No one volunteered. He sighed. Then, Desiree stepped forward. "What do you need me to do?"

He studied her. He would have preferred not to use someone with no experience, but it didn't look like he had much choice. "Okay. Look, this will be easy." He pulled out his four extra magazines and handed her three. "Once I go out there, you stand inside the door, ready to follow me when I call you. Don't delay. I might need the bullets." He turned to Ervin. "Once I signal, you start bringing the furniture through. I'll show you where I want it. Start with that long dresser, there." He pointed. "Don't hesitate. I will only be able to hold them off for so long." Back to Desiree. "When you see me drop a magazine, you hand me the next one. Put the empties in your pocket. Don't lose them." He locked eyes with her to see her resolve. "Can you do this?"

She swallowed hard and nodded. Her face had gone pale.

"Whatever happens, don't panic. I've done this before. We'll be fine as long as you stay calm. However, if I say go, you get your butt back through that door. Understand?"

Again, the nod.

He placed what he hoped was a reassuring hand on her shoulder. Her body seemed to vibrate under his touch. "Relax. We're gonna be fine." He decided they'd better go right then or she might change her mind, or worse, faint. He turned to Ervin. "Ready?"

He looked as nervous as Desiree, but grunted a "yeah."

Evan cracked the door and took a peek. A slow but steady stream of crits moved on the stairs. More than he had hoped, having cleared the area once already. Lifting his weapon, the backup mag squeezed in his left hand, Evan stepped back from the door, lifted his right leg and pounded it into the door.

The heavy door struck a body or two and rebounded toward him, but Evan was through before it closed. Gun up and targeted, he squeezed the trigger in rapid succession. Echoes filled the narrow space, growing in intensity with each explosion. The bodies dropped and piled up in a hurry. In seconds, he dropped one mag and seated the next, sliding the empty in his rear pocket.

With the platform clear, he motioned for Desiree to come out. His bullet count on the second mag had reached eight before she made an appearance. He feared she had lost her nerve. Reaching back without looking, he felt the metal magazine in his palm just in time. He reloaded and handed the empty to Desiree.

The stairwell was cleared to the next platform half a floor below. Only a few stragglers moved above. He motioned for Ervin. The door burst open. Ervin and another man hurried through. In their haste, they got jammed in the doorway for a beat before their adrenaline had them muscling through.

"Put your end against the wall and move it to the edge of the steps. Perfect." Evan guided the placement of the dresser as more furniture was hauled out. During the construction of the barrier, he only had to shoot twice more. In less than three minutes, a substantial and mostly secure barricade had been erected. He finished off two more crits coming down the stairs, then pulled out one box of ammunition and handed it to Desiree.

"Grab an empty mag." He pulled the one from his rear pocket. She reached behind her and withdrew one from her pocket. "Watch closely. This is important." He pulled out several rounds and thumbed them into the mag. "You see this? Same direction. Keep filling until you can't get any more in, then fill the other one. Got it?"

"Yes."

"You did good. I'll need you to follow me upstairs to clear the hall, then down the other side."

She didn't answer and set about her task.

"The rest of you. We need to pick up these bodies and pitch them down the stairs."

One woman squealed, "Ugh! I'm not touching them."

"Get out of the way, Mary," Ervin said, his voice heavy with disgust. He and another man grabbed the first body, counted to three, and flung it over the rail into onto the small group ascending. The body crashed into them and toppled the bunch down the stairs. Ervin cheered. The other man pumped his arm and said, "Strike!"

"Keep it up. Let the bodies build up and act as another part of the barricade. Don't let them get too high next to the furniture, though. The crits will use the added height to climb over." He turned to Desiree. "How you doing?"

She held up the full magazines. "Done."

"Good. Follow me, but not too close."

Taking the steps two at a time, Evan stopped at midflight to see what lie ahead. One crit was on its way down. Evan shot it and kicked it down to the lower level. "Here's another one for you." Climbing to the door, he did a quick peek. About eight undead wandered the hall. *How had they gotten in? Hadn't he closed the doors at both ends?* Someone was probably trying to escape and left the door open.

Without hesitation, he stepped from cover, leveled his gun and advanced. His weapon barked. One by one, the creatures fell before him. He went to the far door just as another crit came through. Evan was in too much of a hurry and walked within its grasp. The crit's fingers dragged across his shirt, snagging in the material.

Heart pounding at the near miss, he stepped back, lifted a foot and shoved the creature away before blasting him. He was so flustered at the near attack and his own stupidity that he fired an extra round into the creature's face.

He didn't have time to clear his head. A group of four was right there. He fought to calm his emotions, but hands unsteady, he wasted two extra rounds to put them down. That angered him. Bullets were too scarce to waste. Even though several more were climbing the stairs, he took the time to change out the mag and lean against the wall. Then he remembered Desiree. He glanced back to see the young woman worrying at her lower lip. Her eyes mirrored the fear he felt. He had to settle down.

You're all right. It was close, but you're all right. Slow down so you don't make another mistake.

He took a couple of deep breaths, then moved to intercept the next wave. Less than thirty seconds later, he had cleared the stairs to the twenty-fifth floor. Standing to the side, he rapped on the door. He didn't want the nervous man to shoot through the door. "Jack, it's me. It's Evan," he said, in case he didn't know who "me" was referring to. The door opened and Jack poked his head out. "It's safe for the moment. Bring the furniture out."

The door was blasted open and Jack and Bob hauled out the dresser. Evan showed them where he wanted it, then dispatched two more crits. Bob clapped his hands over his ears. The shots were deafening.

Working fast, they constructed a wall of furniture, then pitched the dead over the railing. When done, Evan motioned them all back through the doors. Handing the partial mags to Desiree, he leaned against the wall and slid to the floor. The stress of the assault washed away, leaving him physically drained.

Desiree sat beside him. He looked at her, the thin line of her lips the only visible sign of the tension Evan knew she must be feeling. She lifted the extra mags. "Reloaded."

"Good. Thanks."

They sat in silence for several moments before the mob of elite began advancing toward them. Before they arrived, he sensed there was going to be trouble. Unfortunately, he couldn't shoot these problems. He closed his eyes and waited for whatever was to come.

13

"So, what's the plan?" the host said.

"Oh, now you want to know, huh, Hal?" Desiree said. "Thanks for all your help so far."

Some grumbling ran through the crowd. Evan let it go for a few moments to allow himself time to think. Some name calling began, signaling him to intervene.

"Excuse me, young lady, no one is speaking to you," Hal said.

Evan studied the man. He hadn't given a damn about Evan when they'd been introduced, but he had the man's attention now.

"First," Evan said, "someone needs to go upstairs and bring down anyone who is still there. We need to stay together. Not to mention, it would be helpful to know how many people we're dealing with." Hal's wife said, "How do you plan on getting us out of here? Maybe instead of sitting there, you should be finding a way."

The couple's attitude was grating. If he had the energy, he'd stand up and smack them both. "I've taken the first step. The floor is secure. Once we have everyone here, we can put our heads together to come up with a plan."

"Why can't you lead us out of here now?" she persisted.

He forced himself to remain calm. "And how would you suggest I do that? We have an unknown number of crits between us and the ground."

"Why can't you just clear the way, like you just did?" another woman said with surprising attitude.

My God! They're so used to people doing their bidding, they truly have no idea what they were facing. Evan looked at her for a moment before answering, not wanting to snap off a rude comment like he would have, had it been one of his men. "Because I only had about three hundred rounds of ammunition and I've used at least sixty of those already, just clearing two floors. Considering how many crits I've had to deal with on this floor, imagine what it must be like at the lower levels. I'd run out of bullets long before we reached the ground floor."

"What about using the elevator?" Jack asked

Evan sighed. In truth, he'd been wondering that himself. He hadn't run through the pros and cons yet. "That's a possibility, but the car has limited space. With this many people, it might take three or four trips. Where would the first groups down hide to stay safe? Plus, once we got to the bottom, we'd have to have transportation ready, or risk being swamped, not to mention what we might find when the doors opened. We could be trapped in that car with nowhere to run and no room to fight. It might be the best way, but right now, there are some logistical problems that need to be ironed out."

Evan was spared further questions when a small group came through the fire door from the floor above. He stood as they joined the others. Turning to Desiree, he said, "Do me a favor and get a head count. Okay?"

"Sure." She stepped away and began pointing at heads.

An older man moved to the center of the gathering. Evan had never met him, but knew who he was. Martin Welsh ruled the island like he was royalty. He was the voice and the power behind every major decision made in the community. His command and authority were absolute. His minions acted on his words with harsh efficiency. He allowed no one to oppose him or stand in his way.

Still powerfully built, the one-time prize fighter looked like he could still go a few good rounds. An aura of quiet intensity emitted from him. Turning a circle within the circle, he took in the faces as if registering who among them was worthy of his presence and who was fodder.

Behind him was a tall, elegant woman with short blonde hair. Younger than Welsh, his wife Elaine was said to be just as ruthless. Her eyes had a hard edge, ready to shoot fire, destroying anyone in her path. They made quite a formidable couple.

"Who can give me accurate details of the situation?" Welsh said, his voice rumbling through the hall.

The crowd seemed to shrink under the weight of his tone. All eyes swung toward Evan.

"I guess that would be me, sir. Captain Evan Stewart." With a slight hesitation, he offered his hand.

Welsh's eyes never left Evan's. Ignoring the hand, he pointed a thick finger at him. "Are you who we have to thank for clearing the halls?"

"Yes, sir."

"Why are you up here, instead of fighting out on the street, where you belong?"

Evan swallowed his response. Ervin came to his rescue. "Sir, we were just talking about the best way to get everyone safely out of the tower. The captain here was answering our questions."

Welsh seemed to give that some thought before finally saying, "And what have you decided?"

"We hadn't yet come to a conclusion, sir," Evan said. "At this point, there are still too many unknowns."

Elaine said, "Why should we leave the tower? Surely, the defense forces will do their jobs and eliminate the threat."

"They may do that, ma'am, but I have not been able to reach anyone by radio to determine the status. The number of crits inside the compound is staggering. I haven't seen a concentration like this in one place since the early days."

"Well, maybe you need to get downstairs and determine firsthand what we are up against," she shot at him.

Again, he held his tongue, though it was getting harder to do. To his surprise, it was Welsh who tried to calm her. "My dear, I'm sure the captain here is more than ready to go down and defend us. But before we send him on his way, maybe we should discuss some things first."

"Maybe we should ask him why his forces let the crits in in the first place," Elaine snapped. "Someone's head should roll for this. I wonder how close to the top our dear captain here is. Maybe he's to blame."

Welsh turned toward her. Although Evan was unable to see his face, the look he gave his wife was severe enough to make her blanch. She quieted in an instant, but as Welsh turned to face Evan, her eyes flashed at him. Evan swallowed hard. Not a woman he wanted to cross.

"So, give me your professional opinion. Are we safe here, or do you recommend evacuation?"

Evan could feel the eyes of everyone on him. He knew what his gut told him. They needed to get out of there and fast, but other since he couldn't raise any of his troops, he had no actual facts to relay. "Without the benefit of intel, I think we should stay here until first light to get a better handle on what we face. We can begin planning now for either contingency, rather than race unprepared into a dire situation. In the meantime, I will try to gather whatever information I can to better prepare us for what we have to do."

Desiree stepped forward and whispered in his ear. He nodded, then said, "There are forty-one of us. Whatever we decide, it has to be everyone together."

"All right, Captain, I will let you get to it. Report back to me as soon as you return." He looked over the group. "While we're waiting for his recon, I need Hal, Arthur, Ben, Ervin and Jack to meet with me in Hal's apartment to make plans. Everyone else, find someplace to wait—and for God's sake—stay calm."

With everyone dismissed, Welsh and entourage moved toward Hal's apartment. The others scattered, but milled around the hall, their chatter increasing in volume. Desiree stayed by Evan, touching his arm, as if looking for reassurance.

This had not gone as Evan had figured. Jack walked over and offered the gun. "If you're going back down, you might need this."

Evan reached for it, then paused. If something happened to him, they would need the gun, even with limited bullets.

Instead, he retracted his hand, pulled out a spare magazine and gave it to Jack. "If I don't come back, you'll need this."

Jack held his eyes for a moment, then nodded and took the magazine. "Okay, but *when* you return, I'll give it back." He stuck out his hand. Evan took it. "And don't worry about Welsh. We all know what you did for us."

"Thanks." Jack turned and Evan grabbed his arm. "You might want to protect that gun so no one else gets it."

Jack's brows knitted, then a look of understanding lit his eyes. He nodded and walked off to join his boss.

Desiree squeezed Evan's arm. "Don't go. Don't do what King Martin tells you. You might get killed."

He smiled and caressed the side of her face. "I'm a soldier, Desiree. It's my job. I have to do this."

She wrapped her arms around him and hugged tight. "You have to come back. Promise me."

He tried to put some sincerity into his smile. As he bent to kiss her goodbye, he realized for the first time how young she really was. He had been kidding himself with the whole move to the tower and the attention of a beautiful young woman. He planted his lips gently on her forehead and pushed her away. "I have to go. I'll see you later."

He strode to the elevator. The remains of the small crowd parted for him. Some gave encouraging smiles and others said reassuring and cliché words while a few turned and looked away, unwilling to acknowledge him.

Evan unblocked the elevator doors, stepped in and pushed the first floor button. As the doors closed in front of him, he wondered if he would be back again.

14

Teke swung her carbine like a baseball bat, knocking the
first creature down. They were closing in, encircling her. If
she didn't break free in the next few seconds, she never
would. The thought created a sob that stuck in her throat,
making breathing more difficult. The thought of those horrid
beasts taking her down, their nasty teeth ripping her flesh,
was not how she wanted to die. Her entire body shook with
revulsion and fear that threatened to send her into a mental
breakdown. "No!" she screamed, as much to keep her sanity
as to deny the crits. She swung the carbine again, knocking
another one away.

She had run out of ammo minutes ago. She still had her
combat knife, but didn't want to let them get that close to her.
The carbine offered less killing ability, but kept them at a
greater distance from her. Reversing the swing, she missed
the next crit. Her arms were growing heavy. She could not
continue much longer.

As she swung forehand again, she stole a glance. Parker's
weapon lay on the ground thirty yards away, near the bus and
what was left of his body. She had to get clear, snag that
weapon, and find someplace to hide.

With a goal in mind and a slim shred of hope, Teke
refocused her thoughts and increased her efforts. With one,
two, three swings, all making contact and concentrated in one
area, she created a small opening. With one final, clearing
swing, she darted forward, dove low and rolled free of the
ever-tightening circle. She got to her feet and started running.
Only then did she become aware of the pain in her leg. Too
afraid to look and see whether the damage was done by the
contact with the ground or the filthy, clutching claws of a
crit, she ran on, her limp increasing as she pushed her speed.

Reaching Private Parker, her leg gave out and she

stumbled over the bloody remains of the man she had served with for the better part of three years. Ignoring the gore as best she could, it was only as she pawed through his pockets and pouches for extra magazines that she heard the whimper and realized it had come from herself.

She found one spare mag and slid it in her pocket, picked up the AR-15, and bolted past the bus and into the darkness, biting her lip against the pain. Shadows moved in her periphery, but she did not want to look. Able to relegate the pain in her leg to a distant thrum, her gait improved. She pushed on, not sure where to go. She ran long and hard before stopping to see where she was. Her body shook, ravaged by uncontrolled sobs and gasping breaths. She made for the bus, fumbled the keyring from her pocket, and tried every key until she found the one that fit.

Teke stepped up inside, tripped and fell hard as someone or something grabbed her ankle. She rolled on her back, thumping down the step on her butt and fired a longer than intended burst into the crit at the door. As it fell away, she reached up, grabbed the bar that opened and closed the door, and snapped it shut. Teke collapsed into a ball and cried. Her last conscious thought before falling into a complete emotional breakdown was of Evan. If he was still alive, she prayed he would come and rescue her. Then she was gone.

    * * *

To his surprise, the elevator made it all the way to the main floor without stopping. From his perch on the roof of the car, Evan watched as the doors slid open. He waited. Time slowed to a crawl. For long moments, he saw nothing, but then shambling feet and legs came into view. Some walked past, a few peered inside. One sniffed like a dog catching a scent. Evan ducked back and waited. When he looked again, the doors were sliding closed.

Taking a deep breath, he dropped to the floor. He moved to the side of the car and pressed the open door button. Again the doors draw apart. Evan was struck by the eerie quiet. The only sound was the constant scraping of feet along the highly-polished marble floor. His mind formed a picture of how many crits it would take to make the movements audible.

He peeked and ducked back, getting a quick glimpse of the lobby. From his vantage point, he could see a dozen undead. Most were moving. A few were hunched over the remains of what looked like a woman. They gnawed and tore at the flesh. Acrid bile rose to his throat.

Taking a longer look, his head extended out from the car, he discovered the only things moving in the lobby were crits. A scrape to his left gave him warning and he ducked back just as a large Hispanic crit sighted him and moved in his direction. Evan stepped back and allowed the doors to close. He stayed inside for a few minutes, replaying what he'd seen. If the lobby was full of crits, what were the streets like? He had to get to a position where he could observe the outside. The darkness would limit his view, but he could at least get some idea of what they faced.

Evan pulled his knife and once more opened the doors. The crit was standing right there. Evan watched its reflection in the polished stainless steel at the back of the car. The creature hesitated, then entered. Knowing the crits were drawn to sound, he didn't want to attack this one in the hall and risk drawing others to him. Evan plunged the blade through the base of its neck. The creature jerked and danced like a puppet before dropping to the floor. The body flopped several times, unwilling to die. He shoved the body away from the door with his foot and stepped out.

With a chill riding down his spine like an elevator, the doors closed behind him. Evan fought off the brief panic as his escape route briefly shut down, but he shook it off, knowing the doors would reopen when the call button was pressed. He just had to make sure he had enough lead on any pursuit for the doors to close again before any crits arrived.

Gun at the ready, knife in the opposite hand and cupped in front of the trigger guard, Evan moved toward the lobby. If confronted, he wanted to dispatch any crits with the knife as quietly as possible. A gunshot would draw too much attention.

He made it to the lobby. His initial scan swept the large open space, noting the worrisome lack of living. Perhaps fifty crits roamed the once-elegant lobby that was now spattered with streaks, spots, and pools of blood. With a shudder, he offered up a prayer for those taken down by the undead and an additional one that that the empty lobby meant the survivors had all made it to safety.

A large decorative flower pot stood to his left at the side of an assemblage of cushioned chairs. He hid behind the extending ferns. So far, he had been undetected. He waited a beat before moving closer to the doors. The overhead lights outside the doors illuminated a steady stream of rambling shapes and more distant shadows.

The doors stood open, allowing free access for all. Evan looked behind him, then slid toward the opening. He exited the inner doors, then stopped at the outer set as a teenage girl crit turned toward him, extending an arm. He paused. She couldn't have been any older than thirteen or fourteen when alive. He hated confronting the young. It went against all natural instincts. He had to remind himself that any humanity had long ago ceased and she was now nothing more than a wild animal.

He sighed, stepped forward, and buried the blade to the hilt through the eye, giving it a twist before pulling it free with a sickening slurp. The body fell. He stepped over it, moving down the walkway toward the street. Stopping on the curb, he stared, slack-jawed. Nowhere in his limited view did he see a living person. What made the visage more eerie was the lack of sound. He should hear gunshots, running steps, audible signs of struggles, or at the very least, screams. Instead, he was met by the scariest sound of all—silence.

What the hell had happened? Where was everyone? And where had this enormous invasion come from? How could this many crits have accumulated so close to the island undetected? So many questions, no one to answer them.

His attention was drawn to several crits who changed course toward him. He should explore more, but in truth, he'd seen enough. Glancing upward, he tried to locate the balcony he'd stood on only a few short hours before. It was too high and too dark to see. The crits drew closer in their steady shambling gait.

He was about to retreat to the elevator when the sound of a racing engine reached him. He tried to discern where the vehicle was. The engine echoed off the surrounding buildings, hiding its location. He stopped, head cocked at an angle. The noise was getting louder. Evan bolted into the street that ran alongside the tower. Just as he arrived at the corner, a packed pickup truck raced past. The interior was jammed full, as was the bed.

The truck plowed into and over several crits, bouncing as it went. The driver had difficulty holding the course at the speed he moved. As Evan watched, the truck smacked into another walker, tossing the body into the air. It bounced off the windshield, over the cab, and into the people in the bed.

Screams erupted as hands reached to deflect the flying missile, passing it overhead. A man and woman near the back were not lucky enough to react in time. The body struck, flipping them over the tailgate.

Evan watched in horror as the man struck the road head first, the audible snap of his neck louder than the screams. The woman hit on her hands and knees and rolled over and over, stopping not ten feet from advancing crits. The truck kept moving and reached the bridge, its taillights fading into the darkness.

Evan raced for the fallen and dazed woman. He wouldn't reach her before the crits did. Raising his gun, he fired on the run. His aim unsteady, he missed, but kept depressing the trigger. He closed the distance fast, but the first crit was already bending toward its feast. The woman moved, but seemed unaware of her surroundings or the danger that loomed over her.

Evan was forced to slow his speed to make a more

accurate shot. Fast or slow, if he missed, the woman would be beyond saving. He opted for the only chance he had. He braked to a stop, took careful aim and blasted a large chunk from the crit's head. It fell headlong onto the woman. The sudden weight reawakened her. She screamed, kicked, and pushed at the body.

Two more crits reached for her. She tried to scramble away, but a third closed in behind her.

As soon as he fired, Evan started moving again. Within ten feet of the woman, he stopped again and fired twice at each of the undead. Two toppled, but the one behind continued toward the woman. Unaware of its presence, she kept back-pedaling, moving within its reach. It grabbed her by the top of the head, and baring rotted, half-missing teeth, bent to take a bite.

Unable to get a clear shot, Evan sprinted. Just as the crit was about to plant his teeth into the now frantic woman, he took flight over the first dead body, clearing the woman, and crashed into the crit. Leading with the knife, he powered the blade into its upper chest. They went down. Evan rolled away, stopping in a crouch. The knife was gone, so he lifted the gun and fired twice into the beast's head.

He stood, pulling the knife free, and limped over to the woman, who hadn't stopped screaming. More crits were tightening the circle around them.

"Hey! Hey! HEY!" he shouted over her. She quieted for a moment and stared up at him. "Are you hurt? Can you get up?" As he spoke, he changed magazines. "Come on, lady. We need to get to safety." He extended a hand. She paused, but as a crit came into view, she grabbed for him. Evan pulled her to her feet. She gasped and almost collapsed.

"My knee!" she exclaimed. "I don't think I can walk."

Evan fired once. Another crit fell. "You have to do the best you can. If I have to carry you, I won't be able to shoot." He shot again. A quick scan sent a cold bolt of panic through him. Where had they all come from? "You need to start moving toward the tower. Once inside, I can help you, but we have to get there first."

"Okay. I'll try."

One hand holding her injured knee, she began hobbling toward the tower. Evan fired twice more and looked at the woman. At this pace, it would be a long trip to safety.

15

They reached the front doors without hindrance; however, once inside, the undead horde descended. The woman was both physically and emotionally incapable of defending herself. Alternating between sobs and screams, she fell back against the glass entryway. Evan stepped past her, gun barking, and cleared a path.

"Come on," he urged, reaching for her hand. "We don't have much time."

As soon as her fingers touched his, he snapped her wrist in an iron grip and pulled. She cried out in pain, but Evan ignored her. Better a dislocated shoulder than to have it be torn from her body and eaten. He dragged her through the narrow escape route and led her to the elevators. He pushed the button, guessing they would have enough time for the doors to close behind them. But the doors did not open.

Icy tentacles wrapped around his heart. "What the ..." he released the woman's hand and slapped the call button. His mind whirled, praying the next car would come fast and looked for an escape route in case it didn't.

The bank of elevators sat at a dead end. If an elevator did not descend in the next few seconds, they were trapped. Already, the open end of the hall was closing off. More than twenty of the beasts had gathered for the feast. He pushed the button again, aware of his own desperation. Were the cars even still running?

With his free hand, he swept the woman behind him and prepared to defend. "Whichever doors open, you get in. Don't delay. You understand? Hey! I'm talking to you. Do you understand?"

She nodded. Her tears continued to stream as she rubbed her bloody knee.

"You'd better, cause if you don't, we're gonna die. No, let

me rephrase that. You're gonna die, 'cause I won't wait for you."

The creatures drew closer, and now were shoulder to shoulder across the opening. Their numbers grew beyond Evan's ability to count. He readied for battle. Sliding the last two magazines out of his pocket, he tried to do a mental calculation. At best, he had about forty rounds left. He had to make every shot count.

With the distance away from them down to fifteen feet, Evan took two calming breaths and stepped to the middle of the hall. Starting from the left, he fired once and switched targets. All the way across from wall to wall, he placed one round into each crit's head. The bodies began to pile up, yet still they kept coming.

The slide locked back. In practiced seconds, the old mag was dropped and pocketed and the new one slid home. The approaching crowd advanced, shortening the distance. He started shooting again. The numbers were dwindling, but by his estimate, even if the total did not increase, he would run out of bullets about ten short of what he needed.

With cold proficiency, Evan mowed down the next line, switched to his last magazine and chambered a round. Just then, the *ding* sounded, announcing the car's arrival. Relief swept over him. Without looking back, he yelled, "Move!"

Evan gave the woman two seconds, then firing twice more to get some needed room, turned and ran for the open car. He ducked through the sliding doors a moment before they closed. His breath came in short, ragged draws. Staring at the woman, he wondered whether she would've held the car for him had the doors closed before he got in. The look in her eyes told him no.

He went to press the button for the twenty-fifth floor, but discovered this car did not go that far. *Damn!* He pushed twenty, the highest it went. They would either have to switch cars or use the stairs. Either way, he would have to fight. As fast as he could, Evan began thumbing rounds into the empty magazines.

As the car rose, he spoke. "What's your name?"

"I'm sorry. I was so scared."

He repeated in a harsher tone. "What's your name?

"D-Debbie."

"Okay, Debbie. We are gonna try to reach a group of people on the twenty-fifth floor. Unfortunately, this elevator does not go that far. I have no idea what we will face when those doors open, so be prepared." Finishing the first mag, he slid it in his back pocket and pulled out the second empty.

"Stand by the panel. When the doors open, I'll tell you to either close the doors or go. You will not have time to hesitate or think. Do whatever I say as soon as I say it, or we may both die."

The elevator began to slow. He seated two more bullets, leaving the mag three short of full, and moved to the side. The car bumped to a stop. "Ready?"

Debbie whimpered, but nodded.

The doors parted, revealing a crowded hall. Evan raised the gun and shouted, "Close the doors!"

Debbie pushed the button repeatedly. In agonizing slow motion, the doors crept toward each other. They shut without Evan having to fire. He fingered three more bullets from the box and filled the magazine while he thought. They didn't have much choice. "Hit nineteen."

She did and the car responded. "Same routine now." She nodded again.

Once more, the open doors revealed a hallway teeming with crits. "Close."

He waited before giving the next number, wondering if it might be better to go all the way down to the main floor and switch elevators.

"Should I press eighteen?"

"Might as well."

Again, the same results. The next three floors were the same. Now they didn't have a choice but to go all the way down. The two elevators that ran to the twenty-fifth floor did not stop on any floors below fifteen.

"What now?" Debbie asked.

"Now we start all over. Ground floor."

Debbie hesitated. The brief mask of calm she'd been able to hold began to crumble. Her hand shook over the button, but did not touch it.

Evan stepped forward and pressed **G**. "We'll be all right. We just need to move to another elevator. Stay calm and move fast. I think it's the first one to the left as we get out. Stay close. Find the right button and push it." He took her shaking hand and gave it a reassuring squeeze, perhaps more for his benefit than hers. "Hey! We'll be okay."

Before they landed, Evan finished off a box of ammo, sliding a few bullets into a partial mag. It would have to do. The car stopped. "Don't hesitate." As the lobby came into view, Evan stepped into the small milling crowd and began popping off shots. His aim swept in a smooth arc, finding and dispatching targets.

The first mag emptied when Debbie tapped his shoulder. "It's here," she said. Evan was so locked on, he never heard the car arrive. As he stepped inside, he realized they'd made progress. She could have left him there. He blew out a thankful breath and began refilling his empties again.

Now the only question was what he would find on the twenty-fifth floor.

16

With relief, he found the hall still free from crits. He stepped out and found a half dozen people standing around. Seeing him, their faces brightened and they hastened to him.

"Oh, thank God," one man said.

A woman wrapped him in a hug. "We're so glad you're back safe."

Several others clapped his back. It didn't take long for the word of his return to spread. Doors opened all along the hallway and people poured out. He accepted their comments, praise, and well-wishes with a tight smile, but offered little reply other than, "Thank you."

"Everyone, this is Debbie. Would someone see to her injuries, please? She's had a rough ride," he said, aware they would not understand the pun.

Desiree pushed through the crowd and jumped into his arms, knocking him back a step. He caught her and returned the hug. "I was so worried," she said in his ear, then kissed his cheek. Clamping a hand on each side of his head, she looked at him through tearful eyes and said, "I'm so glad you're back." She planted a kiss on his lips, then hugged him again.

"Ah, I hate to interrupt this reunion." It was Jack. "But Mr. Welsh wants you to join him to make your report."

Something in Evan's eyes must have conveyed what he thought about being summoned. Jack threw up his hands and said, "Hey, only the messenger here."

Evan reached behind his head and unclasped Desiree's hands. She lowered her legs to the ground and backed away. "All right. Lead the way."

Jack walked to Hal's apartment and knocked. A crowd followed, but once the door opened, a large man blocked the path of everyone save Jack and Evan. As the door shut behind them, Jack whispered, "That's Otto. He's Welsh's bodyguard. A former heavyweight champ. Careful of him."

Seated around a large dining room table, Evan found Welsh, Arthur Freedman, Ervin, a man named Ben, and Hal. Jack took the empty seat, leaving Evan standing as the subordinate they viewed him as. Heat rose up the back of his neck and creeped around to his cheeks. He forced the anger down. It would serve no purpose. However, he wasn't about to be these power-crazed men's puppet.

"So, Captain," Welsh began. "What is the situation?"

Evan scanned the faces. In spite of the danger that surrounded them, they still wanted to hold court, seeing him as a tool rather than an equal. Perhaps they were right; he was a tool, but he didn't work for them alone. There were a lot of lives depending the decision of this small group of men.

"The tower has been taken over from at least the twentieth floor down. I used an entire box of bullets to get down and back, rescuing one woman on the way."

That announcement annoyed Hal. He slapped the table. "That seems like a waste of limited resources to save the life of one person." He turned to Welsh. "I don't think the captain here is the man who should be holding our precious reserves. Someone with a better grasp of what's important should be our warrior."

The strain in Evan's jaw created a pressure buildup in his head. "Why don't you tell me what's important in your narrow view."

Hal stood abruptly. "You do not talk to me that way. You are nothing but a captain, a position you hold only because this council allows it. You can easily be demoted and replaced and sent to the hall with the rest of the ..."

Welsh slid a hand across the table and covered Hal's, the touch conveying the message to say no more. It was easy to see who wielded the power here.

"Captain, I'm sorry for Hal's outburst. We all appreciate your efforts on our behalf. Let's forget all this for the moment and talk about what our options are here. Otto, would you bring a chair over for the captain, please?"

As the big bodyguard left, Evan watched the quick eye interchange between Hal and Welsh. Evan should have felt some relief at being asked to the table, but instead, felt more tension than before.

Otto returned with a chair and set it down. He gave a smile devoid of all warmth and motioned for Evan to sit. Evan took one step and froze, waiting for the big man to back away. Otto glanced at Welsh and must have gotten the okay signal. He retreated to the wall, but was still too close for Evan's liking. He would have to stay vigilant.

Evan sat but did not pull up to the table. His hand rested on the hilt of his knife. He didn't think Otto would act on his own, so Evan focused on Welsh, sure that any signal would come from him.

"Now then, Captain, give us a rundown of what you observed."

Evan did. His comments were short and factual. He offered nothing more. When asked a question, his response was only the basics. After several minutes of discussion, he began to relax his guard.

"Now that we know what we're up against, what is your recommendation for getting us out of here?" Jack asked.

He glanced at his watch before responding. "The sun will be up in less than two hours. We should be able to see if we can expect any help from outside the building then. We need to gather anything of value, and by that, I don't mean monetary, but of use for our survival. Food, water, medical supplies. Begin readying for a rescue or evac."

"What's your gut tell you?" Ervin asked.

Hal snorted. "His gut!"

Evan ignored him. "My gut says there will be no outside help. From what I've observed so far, we are on our own to survive."

The room went quiet.

"Can you get us out of here?" Ben asked. He was a short,

nervous man of about fifty who couldn't keep his body still for long.

Evan paused and gave it some thought. "If we all work together and come up with a solid plan, I think we can do it."

Arthur Freedman, who'd been quiet so far, leaned his large frame over the table. "What if the number of people you were trying to get out was a smaller, more hand-picked group?"

"You mean make several trips?"

"No, dimwit," Hal broke in. "He means just what he said. A select group. A group of our choosing. The elite. Are you man enough to lead us to safety?"

Evan felt the anger rise. "And what—leave the rest to fend for themselves? He looked around the table, incredulous. Ervin held a shocked expression as well. Jack must have known what was to come, and he avoided Evan's gaze. But it was the opposite end of the table that drew his focus. Welsh, Hal, Freedman and Ben, the elite.

So appalled at what they were suggesting, Evan almost missed the slightest of nods from Welsh. Evan exploded to his feet, kicking the chair backward into Otto's legs. The big man kicked it aside and wrapped his powerful arms around Evan, pinning his arms to his side. Evan had managed to slide the knife free before getting enveloped, but had no leverage with which to use it.

Welsh said, "Jack, relieve the captain of his gun."

"Martin--" Jack said, but was quickly cut off.

"Take his gun, Jack. Now!"

The gun was pulled from the holster. It became harder for Evan to breathe as Otto squeezed tighter. Evan leaned his head back as far as he could and snapped it into the big man's face. Pain ignited like fire in his forehead. Otto shook off the attack, then struck with his own head butt. The blow jarred Evan, sending a white flash exploding before his eyes.

"Otto, please deposit the captain outside."

Ervin stood. "Martin, no! He doesn't deserve this."

"Would you like to join him?"

Ervin stammered but did not respond.

"Remember, we have not yet decided who will be accompanying us. You all need to decide who you stand with."

Evan heard no further discussion. He was lifted off his feet and carried toward the balcony. He wriggled and strained, but breaking free by strength alone was not an option. He tried to twist his head enough to bite Otto's nose, just missing, but the bodyguard evaded the attempt and delivered another devastating head butt that brought a halo of blackness to the edges of Evan's vision.

They reached the balcony door. Otto had a dilemma. To open the door, he would have to release one arm. It might be the only chance Evan would get. He readied to strike in whatever manner possible, but Otto must have felt him tense his muscles. He delivered one more crushing blow with his massive forehead and Evan went limp in his arms.

Otto didn't move for a long moment. Evan, though dazed, was still aware. He feigned a more unconscious state then he was in, but not by much. Satisfied Evan was no longer a threat, Otto switched grips, placing Evan under one arm while he opened the sliding door.

With no more than a few inches to move, Evan positioned the knife and drew the fine-honed edge across the back of the huge bicep. Pressing as hard as he could, he sawed back and forth until he hit something solid. The big man howled and pushed Evan away from his body just long enough to allow him to pull back the knife and drive it into his side. The point hit a rib and skidded sideways.

Otto flung Evan away. His back hit the door frame and bent at a painful angle. The knife went skittering away. Otto clutched at his side and twisted to examine the wound, allowing Evan to get to his knees. Otto looked up, his face contorted with rage. He growled like a wild animal. Knowing his opportunities were few, Evan reacted. He drove off the floor, planting a shoulder into the bulk of Otto's gut. The unexpected attack exploded the wind from Otto's lungs. He staggered backward onto the balcony.

Massive paws descended with amazing force on Evan's back. He almost collapsed, but willed his legs to continue churning. They hit the railing just as Otto used his brute strength to lift him in the air. He twisted, trying to fling Evan over the rail. Aware of his predicament, Evan dropped his legs. Fortunately, his left one banged across the top crossbar and went over. The right leg sought purchase and managed to snake through the iron spindles.

With a Herculean effort, Otto hoisted upward, but the effort sent his own top-heavy weight over the railing. With one leg already dangling twenty-five flights above the ground, Evan plunged a finger upward and into Otto's eye. The big man shrieked and pulled back, minus one eye, which Evan now held.

He flung the orb over the side, dropped to the platform, and crawled toward Otto's legs. The bodyguard writhed in pain, turning circles on the balcony. He bumped into the glass door, rebounded, and as he reached the railing, Evan latched on to both legs and lifted with all his might. By the time Otto reacted, he was already airborne. With desperate swipes by his large hands, he reached for the spindles. One hand managed to wrap around a thin bar, but his weight was too great.

Gravity yanked at his body. His hand slipped, but he still held on. Evan staggered inside, retrieved the knife, and returned to the balcony. Dropping to his knees, he sliced through Otto's fingers. The big man locked his one eye on Evan's face, pleading for mercy, but Evan was beyond granting forgiveness. As the final finger was cut away and Otto disappeared from sight, Evan rolled over and stared skyward, wondering if he would hear the impact.

He did.

17

Evan regrouped. He still had much to do. These madmen would not be allowed to determine the fate of the group.

He stood and did a quick mental check of any hindering injuries, then, knife in hand, started for the dining room.

When he entered, the room was shocked into silence.

"Oh Fuck!" Hal said.

Ben stood so fast, his chair toppled backward.

Jack stood, too, Evan's gun in his hand, hanging at his side. "Evan, you're—you're all right."

Evan thought he heard Ervin whisper, "Thank God."

"Jack," Hal said, "shoot him!"

Jack looked down at the gun in his hand. He lifted it as Evan stepped closer, knife poised to strike.

"What are you waiting for, Jack? Shoot him!" Welsh said. "Shoot him, and your place among us is ensured."

The words had an effect on Jack. Something in his features hardened. Evan took another step closer, although was still too far away to battle a gun. Jack looked from Welsh to the gun, then to Evan. "If being one of you means killing off others for your benefit, I'd rather not." He handed the gun to Evan. Surprised, Evan tensed, ready to spring with the knife and stretched a cautious and bloody hand toward the gun.

"You fool," Hal said. Jack had already set the second gun on the table. Hal reached for it.

Evan snatched the gun from Jack's hand, and in one motion, aimed and fired, sending Hal backward over his chair. He swept the gun toward Arthur and Ben before settling on Welsh. "Anyone else?"

No one spoke for a long while. Recovering his composure, Welsh said, "Okay, Captain, why don't you tell us your plan?"

"You," he motioned at Arthur with the gun, "Sit down. Jack, slide that gun over to me. Don't pick it up, just slide it."

Jack did as he was ordered. Evan picked it up and placed it in the holster. "Now, go open the door and tell everyone to come in."

Two minutes later, the gathered assemblage stood in the living room. Evan allowed the murmurs to continue for a moment, then stood on a love seat. "I need everyone's attention." They began to quiet down, but his patience was at an end. "And I need it right now!" His voice left no doubt as to who was in charge.

"We, as a group, have some important decisions to make. We will do what the group decides. If any of you do not like the decisions that are made here, you are free to do your own thing. No one will stop you, but also, no one will force you to do anything against your will.

"My goal is to get everyone here to safety. It is my belief—not necessarily fact, but my belief—that there will be no rescue from outside. From the little I saw, no organized defense was left, leading me to believe they have all fled or are all dead."

"Could there be other pockets of survivors like us?" one woman asked.

"Yes, that is possible. That's something we will have to talk about, whether to search for others or try to get to safety. Regardless of what you decide, I will try to come back at a later date to search for survivors. It stands to reason that there will be some. My guess is that many were taken by surprise."

"Can we make it out of here?" another woman asked.

"I think so. It won't be easy, but we really don't have much choice. Once the food and water run out, we'll have to move anyway. We don't need to rush our decision. We can hold out here for a time while we plan."

"Can you give us some detail about what we are facing?" asked a man.

Evan nodded. "We have forty-two, well, forty people now. Everyone goes or everyone stays. I won't leave anyone here alone. That's a slower death with no hope. Leaving at least offers hope. All floors are occupied to some extent. Clearing them is not an option. Unless we find other weapons, we do not have enough bullets to do the job.

"The elevators remain an option, but getting everyone down together is a problem, not to mention getting trapped inside if we meet with resistance we can't handle. We would need at least three cars, and only two reach this floor."

Jack said, "What about fighting our way down to the twentieth floor, where we can get three elevators?"

"That's a good thought and a possibility. Those are the kinda ideas we need in order to find the right one."

One woman said, "I don't want you to take this the wrong way, but what about a small group going down to find more weapons? Getting out would be easier then, right?"

Evan nodded. "Again, another good suggestion. That would mean several people would have to volunteer for a dangerous mission. I'm not saying it's a bad suggestion, but it's something we have to think about."

He glanced out the sliding door. A hint of sunlight streaked the eastern sky. "Here's my suggestion for the moment. Gather all the food and anything that will help with our survival and bring it down here. With two full floors clear, we should find ample food and water. We should have a good meal before we do anything. There's no telling when we might get the chance to eat again. Also, wherever possible, you need to change clothes. Find something that you can move freely in; something that will cover as much of your body as possible. Long, heavy pants and long sleeved shirts."

He looked around. "We need to stay as a group and work together. It may seem dire, but we can get through this. Any other questions?"

There were none. "Okay. Let's all meet back here in thirty minutes."

The group dispersed. Welsh and his cronies left and Evan found the room less stifling. He stepped down and came face to face with Felicity. She took his hand and leaned forward. Her lips moved along the side of his face, stopping at his ear. "I'll do anything you want if you get me out of here. Let's go now."

Desiree appeared over Felicity's shoulder. "Who are you kidding, Felicity? You'd do anything he wanted, no matter what."

Felicity stiffened and glared at Desiree. With a last pleading look at Evan, she left to follow her husband out the door. Desiree followed her withdrawal with flame-throwing eyes. When she turned back to Evan, some of the fire remained. "You wouldn't sell us out that cheap, I hope."

"I won't sell anyone out for any price."

That seemed to satisfy her. "I'll go find you something to eat." She leaned forward and pecked his cheek.

He watched her go, suddenly feeling not only exhausted, but old. He turned to face Jack and Ervin. Both men averted their gaze. Evan studied them. Who could he trust? He couldn't do this alone. "So—why support me over Welsh? It's sure to have consequences somewhere down the road."

Ervin was first to meet his eyes. "He's an asshole."

"Not much of a reason."

"We were wrong," Jack said. "I'm sorry."

"Yet you stood by and let Otto march me to my death."

"Yeah, there's no way to justify that."

Ervin said, "That asshole wanted to take a select group of his so-called elite and leave the rest behind."

Evan wanted to ask more; to drag both men over the coals and make them squirm, but if he wanted their cooperation, he had to watch how far he pushed them. He was about to drive another nail of guilt into them, but something Ervin had said changed his direction. "How was he planning to escape?"

"Otto was going to lead us," Ervin said. "He was only taking the men at the table and their wives, a total of ten people. He knew you would be the only obstacle, but honestly, we had no idea he was going to try to kill you."

Evan ignored that part. They still hadn't raised a finger to help him. "Once out of the building, what was the plan to get away?"

Jack broke in. "Welsh and Arthur have yachts anchored across the street from the tower."

That was news to Evan, but the plan offered hope. "Show me."

Jack said, "You mean go down and show you?"

The fear the man displayed annoyed Evan further. "No. Show me from the balcony." His tone held the harsh bite that the man deserved. Without waiting, Evan strode to the balcony, where just minutes before, he struggled for his life. He stepped on the platform and moved to the rail. A chill crawled up his spine, lifting the hairs on his neck and goosebumps on his arms. He placed both hands on the top rail and felt a wave of vertigo wash over him. Fighting the urge to look down at Otto's body, Evan focused his attention on the river.

Jack joined him at the rail. Ervin stayed back. Once more, the hairs rose. His hand slid to the gun and he turned slightly. Jack noted the stance. "Evan, you don't have to worry about us. We're with you—and the entire group. I wouldn't have given you the gun if we weren't."

Evan relaxed a bit, feeling no sense of betrayal in the man's words, tone, or eyes.

"Where are these yachts?"

Jack pointed. "That pier, there."

In the budding sunlight, Evan made out the shape of a long wooden structure that stretched farther into the river than any others. A large, weathered enclosed boathouse stood over the end of the dock, concealing whatever lay within. "Have you seen them. How big are they?"

"Each one can easily hold twenty people."

Evan nodded, the threads of a plan beginning to take shape.

18

Evan stood on the balcony, a ham and egg sandwich in his hands. The sun was halfway up. He studied the streets below, streets that only yesterday were teeming with people, replaced now by thousands of mounds of slow-moving, rotted flesh.

He found what was left of Otto. Like vultures, the crits had swooped down over him, picking his bones clean. Their appetite seemed unquenchable. Evan found their unending need for food strange, if not macabre. Many of them had no stomachs to process what was being devoured. What drove them? Why did they exist? Four years now, and they were no closer to understanding.

"How's the sandwich?" Desiree moved next to him.

"Good. Thank you."

She looked at his hand. With a pout, she said, "Must not be that good. You've only eaten half. It's probably cold by now."

"No, it's fine, really." To appease her, he took a bite. She was right; it had gone cold. Chewing, he added, "I was lost in thought, that's all."

She turned her attention outward. "My God, there's so many of them."

Evan bit into the sandwich and nodded. "That's what's so disconcerting. Where did they all come from and why didn't we see them? It's almost as if ..." he let the thought trail off.

"Almost what?" she prodded.

He swallowed, a task made more difficult since his throat had gone dry. "As if they were organized. Like they had consciously planned this attack."

"What-what are you saying? That those—things can think?"

"I don't know. It seems strange, considering all that we

know about them, but if they were living people, I would think it took great planning to pull this off."

Desiree clutched her arms around herself and shivered. She leaned against Evan for warmth and support. He placed an arm around her shoulders and popped the last bite of sandwich into his mouth.

"Hey, Evan," Jack said from the doorway. "Everyone's here."

"Okay. Thanks." He dropped his arm and wiped his hands together to clear the crumbs. "Let's go talk to the troops."

Inside, the restless crowd displayed their exhaustion and stress on their faces. A pile of suitcases and coolers stood in a corner. *That won't happen*, Evan thought. That's too much to carry when the need was for speed.

Evan noticed Welsh and company stood toward the rear of the gathering. He met Elaine's eyes. Hatred emanated like lasers from her cold orbs. He would find no support from that group. Nothing he could do about it. As long as they didn't cause trouble or attempt a coup, he didn't care what they thought of him.

"I have two possible ways out of here, both with their own form of danger. These are in no way carved in stone. I have discussed elements of each plan with Jack and Ervin, so you know it wasn't just me. I will present them and you can decide. However, whichever way we go, it's important we all go together.

"The first involves getting to the twentieth floor by either the stairs or the elevators. The first groups down will have to fight to clear the floor while the last groups descend. You will be asked to do things you might never have done before, but it is for your own good. Everyone has to make a commitment, or lives will be lost."

He paused there and glanced around the group. He still had their attention, but fear showed on the faces of at least half of them. It was to be expected, as long as that angst wasn't debilitating. He continued.

"If we use the stairs, we go from one side. Using large

tables, we will push our way down through the crits until we reach the twentieth floor. The advantage here is that everyone will be together. The disadvantage is not knowing if any of the crits are still moving once we pass and that I will have to use a large number of bullets. Once on the twentieth floor, we can close the doors and prevent any more of them from entering.

"Either way we choose to get there, we'll have to clear the floor before we can call the elevators and descend together. Once on the main floor, we wait for everyone to disembark and go out as a group. From there, I will have a bus waiting for us. I will have to go down, probably with one other person, and drive the bus to the front. Once on the bus, we will drive onto the bridge. But that's where things get tricky.

"A lot of vehicles tried crossing in the night. Some of them didn't make it and crashed into the barricades. Those cars have created a traffic jam that might be difficult to pass. I think the bus can wind its way through, but there are a couple of spots where we might have to get out and move vehicles to get past."

He studied them again.

"That's escape route one."

He waited for the murmuring to cease. One impatient man said, "Well, what's the other option?" He clearly didn't like that one. In that case, he would hate option two as well, but that was a matter of perspective.

"Two does not involve as much, if any, contact with the crits, but that doesn't mean it's not equally as dangerous." Curiosity crossed many faces. "What it does involve is climbing down the outside of the building."

The crowd erupted in a cacophony of voices on top of voices, creating nothing but loud noise. Again, Evan waited for them to burn off their initial reactions. He glanced at the back of the room and saw Welsh eyeing him with a smirk. Dissension was what he was waiting for. Evan supposed Welsh hoped he would crash and burn, and would then step in and be the savior, except he knew Welsh had no intention of saving any of them.

Jack raised a hand and whistled. The noise abated. "Hey, listen." He raised his voice. "This isn't as crazy as it sounds. Hear him out."

A subtle murmur continued, but Evan talked over it.

"The distance between one balcony and the next is only ten feet. We should easily be able to rig up ropes or harnesses to get us from one to the other. Some of you, once you try it, will discover you can climb down without any help."

The murmur grew again.

"Going this way, we can control our descent and avoid having to fight our way to safety."

"Yeah, until we reach the ground," a man said. "Then what? The first ones down will become targets, drawing the crits to the others before they even touch the ground."

Evan was quickly losing patience.

"Let me finish!" he shouted, his tone more of an order than a request. He stepped forward and the front line retreated, condensing the pack. "I've taken that into consideration. You'll get your chance to comment when I'm done. For now, shut up and listen." His glare had the desired effect.

"While the rest of you are climbing down, I will take another person down with me in advance. We will clear the rooms we will be using at each level. When we get to the ground, we will drive the buses and park them in a line from the bottom balcony to the fence along the shore. We will walk across the roofs to the fence that lines the shore. From there, we will climb over and go straight to the long pier to the left of the tower."

They were all quiet and focused on him now. Evan glanced up and caught Welsh's eyes. He no longer smirked. *Got you, you bastard!*

"At the end of that pier is a boathouse containing two large yachts. That is how we'll get off the island. If we do it right, take our time, and don't panic, we can do this with no crit threat at all. The secret is to help each other."

He paused here, unable to take his eyes off of Welsh. Pure hatred filled the man's eyes. Evan had thwarted his planned escape. He would have to watch his back even more now.

19

After a spirited round of questions about both plans, Evan left and sequestered himself in a bedroom. He didn't want to be involved in the debate or the final decision. If any other plan was formulated, it would be up to them. He let Jack and Ervin moderate the discussion so it didn't appear like the man with the guns was dictating his own desires.

He laid back on the bed, suddenly very aware of his exhaustion. What he wouldn't give for a few hours' sleep.

The bedroom door opened. He didn't look up or open his eyes. It would be either Jack or Ervin, or perhaps Desiree. A click told him whoever it was had locked the door. Now he was betting on Desiree. The thought, despite his weariness and the situation, had a rousing effect on him.

A chilling thought entered his mind. A third alternative was possible. An assassin. He opened his eyes and sat up to see Felicity, her breasts exposed, fingers working the zipper on the side of her pants. She noticed and offered a sensuous smile.

"Felicity, what are you doing?'

"I thought you might enjoy my company for a while."

The zipper made its signature sound. She slid her long fingers into the waistband and began to lower them in a slow, erotic dance of her swaying hips. "You would like some company, wouldn't you?"

Yes, he thought, *just not yours.* "Tell me, Felicity, does your husband know you're here?"

She smirked, reminding him of Welsh. "Why would I tell him?"

"Then let me ask you this. Are you here of your own accord, or did Welsh send you?"

That stopped her with her fingers in the band of her panties. The smile faded. She gave him a hard glare. She fought to put the smile back on her face, but now it looked even more forced than before.

"Why would you think he sent me?"

"Because he doesn't want me using his boat. He was hoping to keep it for himself and a select few. Does your husband know Welsh is pimping you out?"

"I thought you would be different. I thought we could have some fun. We would've taken you with us, then you and I could have continued this on a regular basis." She cupped and lifted her small breasts. "Don't you like what you see?"

He motioned in a downward direction. Felicity smiled, understanding what he wanted. She slid her panties off and stood, showing her full frontal. Evan ogled her up and down, then looked at her face. "Yes, I like what I see very much."

Her smile grew and she started toward him.

"I just don't like you."

She froze. A scowl curled her lips in an ugly fashion. She began pulling her clothes back on. "You're an ignorant man. If you think Welsh will allow you to take his yacht, you don't know him very well. In fact, I wouldn't give two cents for your life. You're going to wish you'd taken my offer." Fully dressed now, she looked at him. Her features softened for just a moment and the real woman beneath shone through. Just as quickly, the hardness returned. She stomped from the room, leaving the door open.

Evan had found out what he wanted. Any doubt that Welsh could be trusted had faded with Felicity's exit. Welsh would try something to sabotage his plans. He didn't know what, but he was sure it would happen.

Deciding he could no longer afford to rest, Evan went into the bathroom and splashed water on his face. Drying with a towel, he stared into the mirror, his thoughts drifting to Teke and wondering if she was still alive. If so, he hoped she was holed up someplace.

He gripped the sink with both hands and made a vow. Once he got these people to safety, he would return and search for her. Desiree was a nice girl, but she was not Teke.

Entering the living room where the majority of the survivors congregated, Evan swept the room. Not surprising, Welsh and his entourage were not present. He wondered what sinister plans they were making. He shrugged off the thought. He could not afford to waste time worrying about them. If they didn't like his ideas, they were welcome to go off on their own, as long as they didn't interfere with his group.

Jack looked up from a roundtable discussion. "Evan, I think we worked out a plan to climb down the building."

Evan smiled. It was good to hear someone taking some positive action. He walked toward the circle. One of the women slid over on a chair and offered him a corner of her seat. He took it. "Okay. Whatcha got?"

"Even though we don't have cable TV anymore, the building was wired for it," Jack said. "I went into one of the bedrooms and ripped a section from the wall." He held up a length of black cable. "It's strong. It'll hold a substantial amount of weight." He looked at Evan for comment.

Evan nodded. "Go on."

"Yes, well, I was thinking, er, we were thinking, that after a few people reach the balcony below, we tie off the end and lower anyone who can't climb down. It'll be long, hard work, but there's no need to rush. We take our time and everyone should make it fine."

"That's good, but first, we need to test the cable to make sure it won't separate. I can do that when I go down to secure the rooms and line up the buses. We'll need several twenty to twenty-five-foot-long pieces."

One man interrupted. "But the balconies are only ten feet apart."

"We'll need extra length to tie off and tie around people," Evan answered. "We'll also need extras in case any do break or are dropped. If this works, I'd like to do two lines at once so we can move faster."

"Why not put a line at each of the balconies?" a red-haired woman said. "We could really go fast then."

"Because to stay safe, we have to clear every room on

every floor on this side of the building. It would take too long and use up the bullets I might need to protect us later. Using just two means I only have to clear two rooms per side."

"Oh," she said, flushing. "I didn't think of that."

"It's okay, Janet," Jack said. "At least you were trying."

"This might work," one of the men said.

"It will work," said Evan.

He stood up and looked at Jack. "I'll leave the cable gathering and the details to you. Make sure everyone is ready to leave when I get back. I'd like to start while we still have daylight." He looked around. "Where's Ervin?"

"He went to get some rest." Jack said. "He figured it was going to be a long day."

"He's right. If all goes well, I should be back in a few hours. Not sure how long it's going to take to get down and back up. I'll take that cable with me." He started away and motioned with his head for Jack to join him. He waited on the balcony. When Jack arrived, Evan leaned on the rail. "Have you seen Welsh and his group?"

Jack shook his head. "No. Not since you made the announcement about using their yachts. You expecting trouble?"

Evan sighed. "Yeah, I think that cagey old bastard has something up his sleeve. It'd be nice to know what, but I can't wait around to find out." He slid his backup gun out and handed it to Jack. "Keep this on you at all times, just in case."

"Won't you need it?" he said, taking the gun.

"As long as I don't do something stupid like drop mine, I should be all right. Besides, it's not so much the number of guns, but the number of bullets. When I'm on the ground, I'm going to do a quick scan for any weapons. Hopefully, I can find enough to arm a few people and give us a better chance."

They stood looking out over the river and surrounding area.

"Hard to believe so much has changed in one day," Jack

said.

"Yeah."

"Do you think we'll ever be past living like this?"

"You mean in a world with no crits?" He shrugged. "I hope so, but it has been four years now."

"How many can possibly be left?"

"Enough to overrun a city of ten thousand."

20

Evan took a few minutes to make sure all the magazines were loaded. He slid a water bottle into a back pocket and two granola bars into a small pack attached to his belt.

"You sure you don't want someone to go with you? I'm certainly willing to go."

"I appreciate that, Jack, but you're the only one I can trust to get things rolling up here. You and Ervin need to get everyone ready and divided into two groups for when I get back. Don't let anyone try to take too much. Climbing will be difficult enough."

Evan bent to tie off the cable. He tested it by tugging on it hard. The knotted encased wire held, but Evan knew the stress put on it during the climb would far exceed his tugging. In truth, he could probably make the climb without the line. He was tall enough to reach, hang, swing and drop, but he had to know the cable's limitations for everyone else's benefit.

"Untie it when I call up."

"How will you untie when you reach the next level?"

"I won't have to. I'll loop it and double it up. When I reach the balcony, I'll just have to pull one end."

"Good luck." Jack extended his hand.

Evan shook it. "And good luck to you. If something does happen up here, try to find a way to warn me."

"I'll do my best."

A small crowd gathered at the door to watch. Evan did a quick scan, but did not see Desiree. He pushed her from his mind and lifted one leg over the top rail, then the other. Slipping his feet through the spindles, he looked down. He could do this. Squatting, he gripped the bars and slid one foot after the other from their perches. He stretched his arms so he now dangled twenty-five floors above ground. Pointing his toes, he sought the rail below, but came up empty. For a brief moment, he felt the unease of doubt crimp his muscles.

He swung in and let his momentum carry him out and away from the balcony. He counted. One. Repeating the process twice more, Evan released his grip on three and dropped to the balcony below. The fall hadn't been far, but the angst of uncertainty caused the jarring to his bones to be more prominent in his mind than in reality.

With an almost-silent, "Whew!" he stood back against the glass door where no one could see him. There he sucked in air fast to calm his racing heart. It shouldn't have been as terrifying as that. At least now, he knew it was easy.

He looked inside the apartment. The shades were drawn but parted in the middle. No one or nothing moved within. He tried the door, but it was locked. That was fine. If he couldn't get in, the crits couldn't get out. Evan walked over and grabbed the cable. Lifting his feet, he hung from the line. Nothing happened. It held. Lifting his legs, he swung back and forth, testing it further. Still, the cable held.

"Okay, Jack. Untie it."

Several seconds later, he heard, "It's loose, Evan. Coming down."

The cable slackened and dropped past him. Evan rolled it up, wrapped an end around a spindle and pushed it through. Repeating the process from above, he stepped over, but this time took hold of the cable. He lowered down, but instead of swinging, grabbed the cable with both hands and shimmied down. He had only made one hand over hand pass when his feet touched the top rail of the next balcony.

Allowing the rail to bear his weight, he breathed easier, knowing the length of time he had to rely on the strength of both the cable and his hands was short. He pulled his gun and tried the glass door. It was locked. Sheer curtains covered the glass, but Evan thought he saw movement inside. He pressed his face to the glass to get a better view. However, nothing became any clearer. Rapping his knuckles on the door, he waited. No one came. He repeated the knock and changed where he pressed his face.

A second later, the horrid, deformed face stared back at him. Evan jumped. The crit scratched at the glass, trying to get at Evan. He backed away and raised his gun, but stopped short of pulling the trigger. If he broke the glass and others were inside, the noise would draw them out. As long as the glass held, they would be safe. He decided to get off the balcony fast so as not to rile up the crits or draw any others to the window.

He yanked one end of the cable and it came flying down. The metal connector end smacked him in the face, missing his eye by less than an inch.

"Ow! Dumb ass! Think before you do shit!"

His face stung. Pulling his hand from the injured area, he saw the smear on his finger. He blotted the spot with another finger, holding it there for a moment. "Okay, bonehead, let's try this again, only smarter this time."

"Evan, you all right?" Jack called from above.

"Yeah, Fine."

He restrung the cable and readied to step over the rail. Then something sparked in his mind. He reached into the pouch and withdrew a grease pencil. On the window, he drew a big X. The marks would serve as a reminder of which apartments were safe. Done, he moved back to the cable and descended to the next level.

Of the following five floors, four doors were locked and one of them had a multitude of undead behind it. He marked each one appropriately. On the floor with the open sliding door, Evan entered and cleared the room. No one was there, but more importantly, no bodies littered the floor.

He cracked the front door an inch and peeked out. The hall was infested. He closed and locked the door, retreating to the balcony. He had just let go of the spindle when Desiree called from above. "Evan, you asshole! Why didn't you wake me to say goodbye?"

"Sorry, Desiree. Didn't want to ruin your sleep. I'll be back in a little while."

"You'd better."

Evan looked down. At least he hoped he'd be back soon. He still had a long way to go. So far, none of the street crits had noticed his descent. Having them waiting for him would not be a good thing. He dropped to the next balcony.

Three floors from there he dropped to the platform and came face to face with a short, squat creature with a chunk of skull missing from above its left eye. The sight took Evan by surprise. He jerked back and started to teeter over the side of the rail. While he fought to recover his balance, the crit snared his leg.

Grabbing onto the cable, Evan hauled himself up with fast and powerful hand over hand pulls. The move righted his balance, but he now dangled above the balcony where the short crit was getting ready to take a bite out of his calf.

Placing the other leg on the top rail, he pushed off, swinging out away from the balcony and pulling the creature with him. As the crit's body was dragged over the rail, Evan brought his free foot down on its head. The crit missed its bite and dropped from the balcony, but maintained its hold on Evan's leg. The added weight threatened to rip his grip from the cable.

He clung tight, trying to kick the being loose, but the crit was not easily put off its meal. It clawed up his leg. As Evan swung toward the balcony, he rammed the creature into the rail. Still, it would not release its hold on him. Clutching the cable in a death grip with one hand, Evan reached for his gun with the other.

Overhead, a woman screamed. Evan was vaguely aware of the onlookers. He brought the gun within inches of the undead head and pulled the trigger. Bone fragments flew like shrapnel, yet the crit held tight. Panic began to overwhelm him. This time, he placed the barrel against its forehead just above the right eye. The explosion blasted the creature off him and down.

Evan's relief did not last. As he hung there, two more crits reached for him. He let out a cry of fear, pushed off the rail, and fired until both creatures fell. As he neared the rail, he wrapped his feet around a spindle, grabbed the rail and vaulted it. As soon as he landed, another crit came through the sliding door. Adrenaline pumping, he fired again. After he felled it, he entered the apartment and systematically eliminated the remaining threats.

Once he reached the front door, he pushed it closed, preventing several more crits from entering. With the entrance cut off, Evan cleared the rooms and collapsed on a sofa. He took out the water bottle and drank half of it down. He wiped his face with his sleeve, then went about exploring. He found the refrigerator held four beers. Evan had no idea where the occupants might have scored such a prize, but however it happened, he was glad they did.

With the beer drained, he dragged the bodies to the balcony and began pitching them over the rail. He was only mildly aware of voices calling to him from above.

He poked his head out from under the upper canopy. "What?"

"Oh, thank God. You are such an asshole!" Desiree shouted. "You had us all worried. Why didn't you answer us?"

"Why don't you stop yelling and drawing attention? In case you hadn't noticed, I was a little preoccupied. Stop watching." Whether his words emanated from fear or annoyance didn't matter. Desiree's head disappeared in a huff, replaced by Jack's. "You okay?"

"Yeah, but people need to stop yelling. The noise will draw a crowd. I don't need a welcoming committee waiting for me."

"I'll see to it."

Evan looked over the rail and tried to count the remaining floors. A sudden wave of vertigo made the count impossible from this height. *Still a long long-ass way* was his best guess.

21

By the time he reached the fifth floor, Evan needed a break. He'd decided to clear as many apartments as he could so there would be room for people to rest. If he was this tired, the others in his party would be exhausted. Of course, they wouldn't have to fight the crits, thanks to him, but still; the climb would take great effort and much stress, especially if they had to dangle with no footing beneath them.

The descent had taken much longer than he anticipated. The sun was on the downside of its apex. The six or seven battles he'd engaged in had absorbed much of the daytime, but at least most of the rooms were clear now and should stay that way as long as no one opened the doors. Most of the rooms below level ten had become infested.

Evan gazed out over the river, studying the horizon. What awaited them on the other side? Was there another undead army massing for attack? He still had trouble accepting that the invasion had happened, let alone been successful. Ten thousand people. Surely they weren't all dead.

One of the major evacuation plans had been for the residents to leave by a multitude of small boats from the opposite end of the island. The various buildings blocked any view of that side of the island, so Evan had no way of knowing how many people had actually escaped via that route. He hoped it was a substantial number; otherwise, a lot of people were now dead.

He glanced at the bridge. A lot of vehicles had tried to cross and failed. He wondered about what happened to the passengers. Had they fled to safety on the other side, or been forced to retreat? To his dismay, he found a sparse but steady stream of crits still crossing the bridge over to the island.

He checked his magazines, reloading where needed. The third box of bullets was emptied, and he let it flutter to the ground, landing a few feet in front of a woman crit. She eyed it for a long time before lifting her head skyward.

Shocked, Evan ducked back. Had that brainless monster just reasoned the box had come from above? What was going on? Had these creatures developed a thought process beyond devouring human flesh? Is that why they were successful in taking the island, because they could now think?

Icy tendrils lashed at his spine. *My God! This changes everything.*

He hadn't really noticed any difference in their behavior or reactions while shooting his way through them. It was business as usual, other than the sheer amount of them in one place. But thinking back, he wondered how had they infiltrated all the floors. Surely, all those doors had not been left open. And how had they been in so many rooms, when no evidence of a human was present in any form, living or torn to shreds? As far as he knew, the crits hadn't begun eating the bones.

Evan began to doubt the success and intelligence of his escape plan. What if the crits were waiting for them on the ground? If one crit heard them coming, was it capable of communicating with the others? He could be leading his charges right to into their waiting hands.

No, he refused to believe it. Besides, it wasn't like they had many other options. They wouldn't survive for long by staying in the tower.

He peeked over the rail. The woman creature was still standing there, looking up. A young boy crit had ambled over. They reminded Evan of the old prank where one person stopped on a crowded sidewalk and stared upward to see how many curious others would do the same.

Flushed with a sudden urge to hurry, Evan moved to the side of the balcony, stepped over the rail and started down. Leaving the cable, he climbed using only his hands. At the bottom of the side bars, he swung a few times before releasing his grip.

Landing in a squat, Evan ignored the wandering creatures

in the room, and without hesitating, climbed over the rail and repeated the process twice more. He now stood two flights above the ground. The duo below still stood watching, but now seemed focused on him. Taking a quick glance in both directions down the street, he noted several other crits in the vicinity. If they joined the first two, his task would be made more difficult. Evan needed to hurry to the ground and eliminate them with as little noise as possible.

Evan was about to step over the rail when the sliding door opened behind him. Surprised, he turned to look, expecting to see another living person. Instead, a host of vile creatures extended their arms toward him.

Unbidden, a cry erupted from mouth. Unable to take his time, Evan vaulted the rail and hung by one arm from the top rail, but it wasn't low enough and he didn't have a good angle to swing for the next balcony. With no other choice, he released his grip just as cold fingers touched his skin.

He plummeted fast. The lower railing was a blur, but he reached for it in desperation. His right hand caught the rail, but his weight yanked him free before he could get a grip. Fingers trailing down a metal spindle, he squeezed tight. His glove parted in a long strip and the skin on his palm was ripped by the metal burs created from years of weathering. Knowing he could not hold on, he thrust his left hand between two rails and bent his elbow, pinning the spindle in the crook of his arm. His downward momentum stopped, but not before his elbow banged against the bottom of the balcony with a painful thud. He cried out in agony, but held on.

His feet dangled four feet above the ground. Fighting through the immobilizing pain, he turned his head in search of the two watchers from below. He could no longer see them, but that gave him no relief. They wouldn't have moved on with a potential meal so near. Then he felt the hands close around his legs.

"No!" he shouted and kicked as hard as he could, expecting at any second to feel the sharp, tearing pain of teeth sinking into his calves. In a panic, he went berserk, thrashing his legs in all directions. He felt solid contact from his right foot. He knocked one of his attackers back. Twisting his body, Evan located the second one. The shorter boy creature barely reached his feet. Evan swung the opposite direction and released his hold on the bars.

He hit the ground and fell backward. Not wanting to be prone with crits hovering over him, Evan forced his body into a back roll, landing in a squat on his feet. He pushed upward, hand withdrawing the knife as he stood. The closed on him from opposite directions. He chose to dispatch the smaller one first.

Ignoring the pain in his palm, he squeezed the handle and drove it hard through the undead lad's eye. The blood on his hand made it difficult to keep a strong grip. His hand slipped, and his fingers smacked into the creature's face an inch above its rotted teeth. He pulled back in revulsion, but no longer held the knife.

He turned, lifted his leg and kicked the woman back. It fell, giving him time to draw his gun. With a few seconds' reprieve, he took in his surroundings. At least another dozen was closing in. He had to end this fight fast and run.

Placing a foot on the boy crit's head, Evan bent and slid the blade free. As the zombie woman struggled to rise, he ran past, burying a round into the top of head. She The body slumped, but remained in a sitting position. The net of pursuit, though closing, had not formed a tight enough circle to prevent him from dodging between them. He leaped over Otto's destroyed body and fired his gun twice more before breaking away. They may be able to think a bit now, but thank God they were still slow. As he raced toward the line of buses, he couldn't help but wonder. *How much longer would it be before they could run like the living?*

22

As he rounded the corner, Evan was surprised to see that only three buses were left of the ten they had. He remembered seeing two wrecked at the island side of the bridge, but that left too many unaccounted for. He prayed it meant a lot of residents escaped safely. He also hoped three would be enough to carry them from the building to the fence. It would be close, but in his estimation they would only be one bus short.

As a scout and collection patrol commander, Evan had keys for three of the buses. They often used the yellow school buses when out on patrol because they were able to carry more troops and more supplies back. Also, the mass of the vehicles was enough to roll over any wandering crits they encountered.

Reaching the first bus and checking his keyring, Evan tried to recall the last time they plowed through more than four of them at once. He couldn't remember, but he knew it hadn't been recently.

The ring held nearly twenty keys, many he'd used so infrequently that he had trouble remembering what they were for. He found the three bus keys together in a row. The bus numbers were written on masking tape wrapped around the head of each one.

With so many buses gone, the odds of still having one of the three he had keys for were diminished, but he had a match for the first one he came to. 567. With a relief that lifted weight from his shoulders, Evan slid the key into the door lock and pushed it open. He closed it, pausing as he saw the bloody palm print on the inside of the glass. For a moment, he stared at it. Then he glanced at his hand and wiped it on his pant leg.

He slid into the driver's seat and inserted the key. The

engine caught on the first try. With a sudden rush for the first time since he started his long climb to the ground, he held a stronger belief that his plan might work. Shifting into gear, he pushed the pedal down and drove onto the road. He accelerated just before he mowed down one crit, then still more as he hit two others.

The distance to the tower wasn't great, so he was forced to slow and merely bounce a few more as he turned the bus facing the lowest balcony. The tires bumped up over the curb. He slowed to a crawl and edged the hood toward the balcony. The bumper and about three feet of the engine compartment squeezed under the bottom of the platform before scraping. Evan shut the engine off, exited the vehicle and locked the door.

Before any crit could get close to him, he was running. When he reached the final two buses again, he checked the keys. 248 and 419. *Damn!* He didn't have either key. He would have to break in and hotwire the engine. The downside was that he wouldn't be able to lock the door, but once they were in place, that shouldn't matter.

He scanned the ground until he found a good-sized rock. He threw it at the window in the door, but it ricocheted back without even causing a crack. He tried again, this time as hard as he could throw. A long line formed and crawled up the door, but still the glass held. As he picked it up for a third attempt, he noticed he'd drawn the attention of several more crits. He had to get inside fast.

Evan decided to hold the rock this time and pound it into the glass until it gave way. He brought his arm back and punched. The impact created a vast spider web, but also sent shards of pain lancing up his arm all the way to his shoulder. He shook off the aftershock and reared back again. This time, just as his arm shot forward, as if by magic, the door opened. Unable to stop his momentum, he was launched inside the bus and fell up the steps.

"Finally, he falls for me."

Evan looked up, still confused, until he saw the smiling

face of Tequila Lopez. His heart danced. A lump formed in his throat. He'd never been so elated to see anyone. He swallowed, finding his voice. "Teke!" He scrambled to his feet and raced up the stairs. Without thought, giving himself to the elation at seeing his friend alive, he scooped her up and clutched her body to his like she was a rag doll.

"Oh my God, I'm so glad to see you." He squeezed her tight. "I feared you might be—" he choked on the word.

"If you don't lighten up and stop molesting me, I still might be."

He loosened his grip enough that her feet touched the floor, but he wasn't ready to let go of her yet. She pushed back and looked at him. "Holy shit! Is that a tear?" she chided.

He let go then and fought for composure. "Hell no! A tear? What? For some skinny little grunt like you? Some crit poked me in the eye, that's all."

"Whatever!" she said, a twinkle lighting up her eyes. In a flash, her gaze went hard. Lifting a foot, she kicked the bar that closed the door as a body slammed into the glass. Another followed.

"As glad as I am to see you, Stu, what's the plan?"

"I need to move this bus." He saw her weapon on the seat. "You loaded?"

She shook her head. "I got three rounds." She found the bullets loose in her pocket.

"We'll have to make do. I've got about forty people trapped on the twenty-fifth floor. I need to get them down. I'm trying to create a wall from the lowest balcony to the fence so we can run along the tops and jump over the fence. We're gonna make our escape using two yachts in a boathouse."

"So, is one of these…people we're rescuing your new girlfriend?"

"Don't start, Teke. Lives are at stake."

She averted her eyes at the reprimand and sucked in a long breath. "Okay. So we get them off the island. Then what?"

"What do you mean? We find someplace safe to hole up for a while."

"No. I mean, what about the other people who might be stranded? Do we just save your rich friends and forget the rest?"

He paused, trying not to respond before his anger subsided. "You think so little of me now? Do you really think I'd ever do that?" The volume of his voice rose and the words shot out like bullets. "Don't sit in judgment on me, Corporal. I'm not that far gone yet. Once they're secured, I plan on coming back and finding as many others as possible. I had planned to do that by myself since I didn't know if any other troops were still alive. And at this moment, I don't care if you go back with me or not. Now, get out of my way. I need to move this bus."

She stood aside and he jumped into the seat. He bent low, looking under the dashboard for the wires he wanted. Next to his ear came a jangling sound. He turned his head to see the keys. "It might be easier if you use these." He straightened and took them. She held on for a moment and their eyes locked. The anger flushed out of him. Offering a slim smile, he nodded his thanks and she released the keys.

"You might want to hurry," she said. "The natives are getting restless, and by the looks of it out there, the dinner bell has sounded."

Evan looked through the windshield. To his surprise, the number of crits had swelled near fifty. He started the engine, revved it a few times, then pressed the pedal to lurch the big vehicle forward. Several crits clung to the grill. Most fell off, some became speed bumps. One began to climb hand over hand up the grill facing and onto the hood.

Stunned by the creature's determination, Evan could not take his eyes away. "Something is very different about them. Have you noticed?"

"The only thing I've noticed is that they die just like always."

"Pay better attention, Teke. They actually seem to have developed a basic thought process. It's a little scary."

The bus picked up speed and pulled away from the pursuit. However, the distance they traveled was not far enough to be out of the sight of the crits, still following. The return trip for the third bus would be more difficult.

Evan pulled the bus around and backed toward the first. Under Teke's guidance from the rear window, he parked bumper to bumper. He shut the engine down. "We have to get out of here before they get too close and we have no room to maneuver around them," he said.

"We've got some coming from the other side now, too." Teke pointed with the barrel of her carbine.

They exited and Evan locked the door. They ran a much more circuitous route than intended to the third bus. The pursuing crowd had grown to the extent that they couldn't just dodge through them. Running along the fence, they reached the last bus and climbed across the back bumper pressed against it. Noting the keys were unmarked, Evan tossed them to Teke. "Find the right one. I'll hold them off."

Teke struggled through the ring key by key, swearing under her breath with each failure. Evan didn't want to waste any bullets if he didn't have to, but as the horde drew ever nearer, he tensed his trigger finger. Lifting the gun, he aimed at the closest crit. To his relief, Teke gave a triumphant, "Yes!" and pushed the door aside.

She entered with him close behind and jumped into the driver's seat. Evan closed the door and held the bar in place as a growing number of crits tried to get at them. This bus, however, was not as cooperative as the first two. The starter cranked; the engine sputtered. Teke tried over and over until Evan feared the battery had been drained. Teke slapped the wheel. "Come on, you oversized minivan. Start, or I'm putting a bullet in your sorry ass."

Heeding the threat, the engine caught. When Evan looked back, he saw Teke kissing the wheel. She dropped the stick in gear and fed the gas, and the bus began to roll. Just as they reached the street, it conked out.

"Ah! You bastard!" she shouted. "Start, damn you! Start!"

This time when the engine ignited, she revved it for almost a minute before putting it in drive. She accelerated fast, adrenaline pushing her hard. "How do you want this one?" she asked.

"Nose first. I want the highest point facing the fence."

The existing space was limited for a turn, so it took several attempts before Teke could park in a way that would allow a smooth run from bus to bus. She turned the engine off. "Now what?"

They only had about a minute before the crowd would arrive for dinner. He walked fast to the rear of the bus and looked out the window. About a four-foot gap existed between the end of the bus and the fence. They would have to jump. He did a quick calculation, evaluating who could make it on their own and who would need help. A few of the bigger men would have to get over first and catch or aid the others. Not perfect, but still better than it had been.

"Ah, I don't want to nag, but if we're supposed to get out of here, we don't have much time."

"Yeah, let's go."

He hurried back. "We're going up on top and to the tower." He looked at her. "Ready?"

"Always."

With Evan on the steps, she opened the door. As soon as the space appeared, it was filled by a large, disgusting beast. Evan shot him and the next nearest two before he had room to get out. He covered Teke as she scampered up on the bumper to the hood before following her up.

She hoisted her body up to the roof, where she dangled for a moment. Evan thought about helping her from behind, but knew she wouldn't appreciate the assistance or where he would have put his hands to push. Once she managed to slide a leg on top, the rest was easy.

Eager hands stretched for him as he placed his palms flat to the roof and pressed upward. One hand brushed his shoe as he raised it, but otherwise, he attained the roof with no complications. He started along the yellow roadway to the balcony. There, he jumped over the rail and waited for Teke to do the same.

"Okay, that part was easy. Now what?" she asked.

He pointed up. "Now we climb."

"Ah, yeah, no—I don't think so."

"You afraid of heights there, Corporal?"

She sneered at him. "Don't be an ass."

He flashed a quick smile, then was all business. "Here's what I need from you. Keep this room and balcony clear. Try not to engage unless necessary. Stay out of sight so as not to draw too many crits. I'm no longer sure what they're capable of doing." He remembered the balcony above. He flashed back, focusing on the sound of the sliding door opening. Was he sure the door was closed, or had he been so tired that he hadn't checked? If it had been closed, it meant one of the crits knew to pull it to one side to gain access to the balcony. The thought terrified him. They were beginning to problem solve. As if surviving these things wasn't difficult enough already.

"I have to climb up. The balcony above has active crits. I'm gonna have to clear the room before I lead the others down. The cable I used to descend much of the way is still tied to the fifth floor railing. Once I get there, I'll toss it down. Try to catch it, but if you miss, don't go after it. We can always rip more out of the walls.

"Once you have the cable, figure out a way to tie it off and climb up. Each room should be clear, but check them for any possible weapons. We're really short on those. Questions?"

She worried at her lower lip, eyes darting from one spot to another like a drug addict.

"Okay, then. I'm going."

Before he could step to the rail, she launched herself at him, stretched, snaked a hand behind his neck and pulled him down. She pressed her lips to his in a hasty kiss. She released him, their lips parting with a smack. She held his eyes. "Not how I envisioned our first kiss, but I had to. You know, just in case."

He smiled and tried to pull her back, but she squirmed away. "Nope. Sorry. One per customer. Besides, what kind of girl do you take me for?"

"The kind I'd like to kiss again."

Color flushed her cheeks. "Well then, come back down safe and we'll see about another."

He smiled. "Deal."

Evan placed a foot on the rail and pressed upward, rising to his full height. Something tugged at his pant leg. At first, he feared the crits had learned to climb, but when he looked down, he saw doe-eyed Teke standing there. "Hey, I'm serious. You come back safe."

"I will. You just be here when I do."

"Deal."

Evan reached overhead, grabbed the lower section of the spindles, and pulled himself from view.

23

As soon as he cleared the platform, he came face to face with the female crit who evidently had been waiting for his return. Sitting on the deck, a spindle clutched in each hand, it bared vile teeth and lunged forward to bite his fingers. The move shocked Evan to the point he almost let go of the bars. However, even though the woman creature had been able to reason out where he would be, it had been unable to understand the metal bars would be in the way. Its forehead *thunked* into them, blocked from obtaining a flesh treat.

Evan lowered his body until his feet found the next railing. Then he sidestepped to the right until he was against the building's exterior wall and climbed again. The woman thing hadn't moved, other than to press its face to the bars in an attempt to see where Evan had disappeared to. Though they seemed to be capable of the basic thought process, they weren't very good at it yet.

This time, Evan pulled himself up as fast as he could and slid one leg on the narrow ledge outside the rail. Balanced, though precariously, he released the top cross bar from his right hand and pulled out his gun. Ten crits patrolled the balcony. He would have to eliminate them all, as well as any inside to ensure the safety of the party when they climbed down, providing they ever got this far.

Having drawn immediate attention, Evan took quick aim and began firing. Round after round blew through the rotted skulls of the undead creatures. Bodies toppled in a pile. The squatting woman crit stood and reached for him. It was the last one on the balcony. He knocked the arms aside with his gun, then pistol-whipped the side of its head. The force of the strike flipped over the rail and to the ground. He stared down at the body, which had landed in a large bush, one of the branches puncturing the abdomen and holding it in place.

The arms and legs moved like a child making a snow angel. He watched for a moment as the undead eyes found his, then stepped over the rail.

Several minutes later, the room was clear. One by one, he dragged the twice-dead corpses to the rail and pitched them over. After tossing one body, he caught sight of Teke looking up at him, her expression grim.

"You okay?"

He nodded and finished the cleanup.

Once the room and balcony were uncluttered, he barricaded the front door, closed the sliding balcony door, and scaled to the third floor. Unless something unforeseen had happened, which by now he knew was a possibility, the remaining balconies should be safe.

Reaching the fifth floor, he untied the cable and called down to Teke. She leaned over the rail. A small crowd of crits had gathered around the balcony, trying to reach her through the bars. He dropped the cable and she snatched it. A crit managed to snag an end, but she tore it from the grasp.

He worried about her trying to climb up, but refrained from calling down a "be careful." She would've resented that. Instead, he turned his attention to the climb that lay ahead of him. He shook out his arms and shoulders and wondered if he would have the strength to make it all the way up and back down again. *Can't think about it. Just start climbing.*

For the next thirty minutes, he kept his mind clear and muscled his way upward. With each floor he climbed, his energy and strength were depleted, making his progress slow. Once, he stopped and leaned over the rail to catch his breath. Below, he noticed Teke pulling herself up the black cable to the third floor. The sight brought him relief she was safe and the spark he needed to continue.

As he lifted his leg to step over the railing of the eighteenth floor balcony, he heard a gunshot from above. He flinched reflexively, then looked up. A second shot followed along with muffled screams. A shard of panic pierced him. He could think of only two reasons for gunfire. Either the crits were up there, or Welsh and his cronies had tried to take Jack down.

Adrenaline pumping renewed energy, Evan climbed faster now, desperate to reach the top. *What would he find when he got there?* If Welsh had been successful in wresting the gun from Jack, he might be waiting for him to poke his head above the rail. Evan had no doubt the man would prefer him dead. He had no choice. Regardless of what he might find, the others were counting on him to get them out of the tower. Concern for his own safety was not a consideration.

At the twenty-fourth floor, Evan stopped and entered the apartment. He walked to the front door to listen, though he didn't expect to hear much. Opening the door a crack, he peered out. To his surprise, the hall was almost empty. He pulled the door open wider and poked his head out. The last crit on the floor was passing through the open fire door at the far end of the hall. *What?*

He stepped into the hall and followed. At the fire door he stopped and glanced, pulling back immediately. A steady flow of crits was parading up to the twenty-fifth floor. Had they found a way through the barricade? Then, he froze. An icy fist squeezed his heart. Had someone purposely opened it for them? Evan backtracked to the other fire door. There were crits, but not as many as he'd anticipated. Making a hasty decision, he slid the knife out and went through the door. He knifed his way upward, trying not to use the gun for anything other than for a club. He didn't want to shoot if possible and announce his presence, in case Welsh had taken the gun and was waiting.

He reached the turn. Above the barricade, things looked to be in place. Six crits bounced around each other like pinballs in a machine. Evan took the steps two at a time. Grabbing the back of a tattered shirt, he yanked backwards and sent the creature sprawling down the stairs. He drove the knife through the side of another's skull and kicked a third down the steps.

Before the other three could close on him, he vaulted over

the barricade and opened the fire door. His eyes almost popped from his head when he saw the herd of crits on the floor. But not only were they on the floor, they appeared to be huddled around the door to the unit where the party had been. Where were Jack, Desiree, and the others? Without hesitation, he lifted his gun and began blasting his way down the hall. He had never fired so fast. The first magazine emptied in seconds, and the next was inserted and ejecting cartridges almost without a pause.

Evan had to be careful as he advanced. The bodies were piled up so high that his footing was unsure, but he could not afford to look down. To lose track of the massive horde for an instant would mean his life. He ejected the second magazine, missing it as it fell to the floor. Halfway through the third, he reached the door he wanted and kicked it without breaking his shooting rhythm. No one responded.

He kicked again, this time risking a sideways glance. "Anyone there? Open up. It's Evan."

The steady gunfire was so loud, if someone had responded, he couldn't hear them.

The third magazine went dry and he slammed home the fourth and last one. If the door didn't open soon, he would have to retreat. The spent shells ejected in a stream, tapping a cadence off the wall. He kicked and shouted, but still no one came. The crits kept advancing; however, their progress had been slowed by the massive mound of bodies before them. His heart felt as if it would explode from his chest. The expelled gases burned his eyes and nose. His throat had gone dry, making both breathing and swallowing difficult.

When the slide locked back, he looked at the door, pounded his fist and screamed, "Open the fucking door!"

He began thumbing rounds into the magazine as fast as possible, dropping as many as he seated. About to give up and retreat, he heard a scraping sound on the opposite side of the door, as if something heavy was being dragged away. Frantic shouts came from within. The door chain rattled and the door was pulled back. However, something was blocking it. He put his shoulder into the door, but it only moved an inch or so.

The crits were beginning to crawl over the fallen bodies. Just then, Desiree's face appeared in the crack between the door and frame. "Evan! Help!"

Beyond her, Evan saw a crit. Somehow, one of the creatures had gotten inside the apartment. As it reached for her, Evan stuck his left hand through the opening and put it on top of her head. He shoved her down hard, pushed the gun forward, and pulled the trigger. It took two shots to drop the beast.

He released her head and she sprung up like a whack-a-mole. She screamed and pawed at her head and body like a spider had just dropped on her.

"Desiree! Desiree, are there any more?"

"What? What?" She was hysterical.

Evan reached through and grabbed her face to hold her still. "Are there any more crits in there?"

"No. No."

He let her go and she slumped against the door, weeping. Evan had no time for this. He had to get inside. Turning, he fired his last four rounds, increasing the size of the mound. He dropped the magazine and started to reload as he said, "Desiree, I need to get inside. Can you get someone to help you clear the door?"

"Yes. Yes. Yes." She turned, disappearing from view. Evan eyed the still-advancing creatures and wondered if she would return.

24

While he had a moment, he finished loading one
magazine, then bent to retrieve the dropped one and as many
bullets as he could find. He finished loading the second one
when Ervin came to the door. "Oh, thank God you're back.
Help me here," he said to someone unseen.

A few beats later, the door was open wide enough for him
to squeeze through. As soon as he was inside, Ervin and
another man shoved the furniture back against the door.

Evan collapsed into a lounge chair. The other man walked
down the small hallway and knocked on the doors. People
emerged with caution. He saw two other crits on the floor
and looked up at Ervin. "What the hell happened?"

The big man stiffened. "Welsh happened."

The crowd gathered around him, everyone talking at once.
Someone put a bottle of water in his hand. He drank it down
and waited for the cacophony to end. Finally, Ervin had to
shout to quiet everyone. Too exhausted to stand, Evan looked
up. Without having to repeat the question, Ervin began the
explanation. "Welsh managed to convince a few of the others
to join him. Unaware of their new allegiance, they managed
to sneak up on Jack and me and take the gun. Jack was shot
in the process."

Before he could ask, Ervin raised a hand to stop him.
"He's wounded, although I doubt they were shooting with
that intent. Took a bullet in the side. The doctor treated him,
got him bandaged and resting, but," he shrugged, "who
knows how he's really doing?"

A woman broke in. "What are we going to do?"

Another woman responded, "Let Ervin talk."

The crowd mumbled, but no one else spoke up.

Ervin continued. "The bastard took a small group of
people and left. He also took most of our food and water and

the cables we'd ripped out of the walls, and then told some of his group to take down one of the barricades."

"The rotten fucker," a woman said.

"And, as if that wasn't bad enough," said a man, "the bastard left us defenseless with the door open, then took off."

"The motherfucker doesn't care if we died," another woman shouted, then covered her mouth to smother a sob.

Ervin started again. "We had no way to defend ourselves, but we couldn't afford to let any more of those things in. A few of us played rodeo clown, distracting the beasts, while the rest of us got to the door. We closed and barricaded it; managed to kill two, but had to retreat to the other rooms to avoid the one you shot."

Evan spoke. "Did he give any indication of how he was getting out of here?"

"I'm not sure, but I think they were going to climb down like we were. At any rate, they took the cables," Ervin said.

"They might have wanted to stop you from getting down."

"I don't understand why they couldn't work with us."

"Men like that don't work with peons like us," a man said.

Evan said, "They didn't want to share the yachts." He stood abruptly, realization of what he just said sinking deeper. "We have to hurry. He's going to take both yachts and leave us stranded."

That announcement caused a panic. Evan stood on the chair and shouted, "Settle down, now. Your anger and silly chatter will not change what's happened. The only way to get out of here is to resolve to do so. We need to work together and do it now. We need more cable. I have cleared the rooms beneath us all the way down to the street. The buses are lined up. We are ready to go, but we need to get organized and do it this instant.

"Do not panic. Do not rush and end up getting someone killed. We will work methodically and as a team. No one is going to be left behind. Do you understand?"

He got a lot of wide-eyed nods.

Desiree said, "What about Jack?"

Evan paused. "We're gonna have to rig something together to lower him down. Ervin, will you and Desiree see to that?"

He nodded and moved off.

"For the rest of you. How many think they can climb down without the aid of a cable?"

Five hands went up.

"Start now. Climb down, take the kitchen knives, and begin ripping cable from the wall of the unit below us. Please do not go down any farther on your own. There will be others who will need your help to climb down. This is not every man for himself. Go."

Those five went to the balcony, others watching them go. Evan did a quick estimate. Without Welsh's group, their number had dropped to about thirty. Still a lot and certainly too many for one yacht, but they could deal with that once they got everyone down.

"How many think they can get down with minimal assistance?"

The majority of the hands went up.

About five people felt they couldn't do it at all, four women and one man with a deformed arm. A large woman broke down in tears and collapsed to the floor. "I can't. I can't. You're going to leave me behind. I know you are."

Evan bent and took her arms. In a stern voice, he said, "Get up. We won't leave you behind unless you sit around, feeling sorry for yourself. Everyone goes, but you have to make the effort. No one wants to die helping you get down. You have to try and try hard. You understand me?" He stopped suddenly, realizing he had not only been yelling at the woman, but shaking her, too.

Her tears fell, uncontrolled. He pulled her head to his chest and hugged her. "I'm sorry." Then he helped her up. "We are not leaving you. Get that thought out of your head." He turned to the group. "I won't lie; this will not be easy, but it can be done. Besides, there isn't any other option. You have to believe you can do it. Once you get down a floor or two, you will see it's easier than you think. From there, it will just be a matter of time.

"Now please, everyone. Get prepared to go, mentally and physically."

He walked toward the hallway. He entered Jack's room to find the man sitting up. His pale face was contorted in pain. "Hey, buddy, you up for this?"

Jack seemed to relax. "Man, I'm sorry. I should've known Welsh would be up to something."

"Put it out of your mind. We've got a lot of work to do."

"He's insisting he can do it on his own," Ervin said.

"That's good, Jack, but by the time I got down there, I was exhausted. You can help as much as you can, but you also have to conserve your energy." He turned to Ervin. "Work up some sort of harness for him. He can climb, but at least he'll have support, should his strength give way." Back to Jack. "That's the best and safest way. All right?"

"Yeah." He winced as he slid off the bed and tried to stand. Desiree caught him and lent her shoulder for support. Concern shone on her face. "I've got you, Jack. Let me help you."

Ervin came back from the closet with a handful of leather belts. "These might work."

Evan patted him on the back. "Good man. Get him rigged up. I've already started some people down."

Back in the front room, he scanned the group. Everyone was in motion and the chatter volume was low. That was good. No panic—yet.

He went out to the balcony and peered over the rail. A man climbed up on the rail below. He held a roll of black cable. Evan bent and extended a hand through the bars. "Here, pass it up." The man did as he was told. "Get ready," he said. "I'm going to pass the first person down."

"All right."

"Send two men to the next level for more cable and to catch the next batch." He went inside and found the heavy woman. He smiled as best he could. "You ready?"

She backed away, her face going bone white. "No, start

with someone else."

"No, you're first."

"Why? You need a guinea pig? If it doesn't work and I fall to my death, oh well, so what? At least the fat girl is out of the way."

Evan sighed. In a rush, he closed on her, wrapping his arms around her. She tried to struggle, but he squeezed the energy out of her. With his lips next to her ear, he whispered. "You listen to me or I'm gonna throw you off the balcony. You have one chance and one only. I need you to show everyone else that it can be done. Once you make it safely to the next level, you and everyone else will be fine. We'll move much faster than they will. Do you understand?"

She sobbed, but did not reply. He shook her. "Answer me, dammit."

"Yes."

"What's your name?"

"Helen."

"Helen, you are not a sacrificial lamb. You are the shining example to all that it can be done. I need you. The group needs you."

"Okay. Okay. I'm just scared."

"I know. We all are, including me, and I've been down once already. Now, let me get you ready." He stepped back and wound the cable around her arms and around her body. Done, he looked her over and feared the cable wouldn't be enough. He looked around the room, lighting on a wooden dining room chair. He had an idea. He went back to the balcony.

"I need more cable!" he shouted.

The same man poked his head out and said, "Coming." He reached below, took a roll from the man on the twenty-third floor and passed it up. Evan had about twenty feet to work with. Back inside, he slid the length under the chair, then wrapped it around the legs, the arms, and the back. Satisfied, he walked back to Helen.

"This will be easier than I thought, Helen. Let me show

you." He explained the process and led her to the balcony. She shook visibly when he said it was time. He lifted the chair over the rail, balancing two legs on the ledge. Ervin and another man took the cable ends of the chair while Evan and a fourth man had Helen's lines.

Evan helped the reluctant woman up on the rail. "Now, lift your legs over the side. Put them on that ledge right in front of the chair. Come on, you can do this. We've got the cable holding you." Using his body, he nudged her off the rail. She gripped him around the neck, not letting go, threatening to haul him over with her.

"The ledge. Put your foot on the ledge." He squeaked out a strangled command. It didn't help that the heavy woman was also short. Once on the ledge, he told her to take one hand at a time off his neck and grab the rail. He had to pry them loose. "Helen, you have to help us. There. See. Now lower your butt and sit." She did so with only mild whimpering.

Evan shouted below. "Are you ready?"

"Yes. We've got her. Pass her down."

"Okay, Helen. Grab the bars there." He showed her. "Remember, you have to help. You will only be in the air for about five feet, maybe three seconds. Do not panic."

"Easy for you to say."

"Yes," he smiled, trying to sound confident, "it is."

Helen screamed as the four men lifted her in the chair and she began the descent from the ledge. At the bottom of the platform, she had a death grip on the spindles. "Helen, we can't hold you forever. You have to let go." Ned, who was waiting below, saw the impending doom and climbed up on the rail and talked her into letting go. As the strain grew unbearable, Helen landed safely.

Evan turned to the watching crowd and heard the unison exhale. "See how easy that was? Who's next?"

After lowering several more people and finding a rhythm, more cable was passed up and they started lowering two at a time. They were also able to lower people by two levels at once, but due to the lack of confident catchers and free climbers, two was only as far as they could go.

More than two hours later, the entire assembled party, including Jack, sat resting on the twenty-third floor.

25

With daylight fading, Evan said, "Okay, now that everyone here knows they can do it, we need to step up the pace. I don't want to do this in the dark. We may have to finish in the morning, but I want to be at least four more floors down by the time we quit. So step it up and let's get moving."

This time, after climbing down once, two more people thought they could make the next climb unaided. Helen's move still took some time, but it was much better. Jack insisted on being lowered like anyone else. With the initial fear behind them, the descent went much smoother. After four more floors and darkness now full, they took a vote whether to try two more levels or rest. Rest won.

Evan hated to stop, but he wasn't going to argue. His body screamed for a break. Before anyone's strength gave out and sent someone else plunging to their death, it was best to stop. What was one more night? His only fear was not knowing what Welsh was doing. By the morning, he might be long gone, taking the yachts with them. Evan contemplated going down to keep watch, but decided he was too tired.

He watched Desiree dote on Jack and smiled. Then his thoughts turned to Teke and the kiss. The memory was broken when Ervin sat down next to him. "So, what do you think?"

"About what?"

"Our chances, for one thing."

"I wish we'd gotten farther, but it's going well so far."

"I'm just glad no one fell."

"Yeah, I'm with you there."

"What do you think Welsh is doing?"

Evan paused, then said, "I wish I knew. I can't see him staying up there, but unless he knows some secret way out, I can't imagine."

"Maybe he's gonna try the elevator and run for safety."

"Could be. I'd given that some thought, but with a group this large and only one gun, I didn't like our chances. No matter how well we planned, someone would probably trip or get separated. We'd lose people and I don't want to risk it."

They sat in silence for a long moment before Ervin spoke again. "You know, while you were gone, there was a lot of talk about whether you'd come back. A few started talking shit and the paranoia spread."

Evan turned to the big man. "And what did you think?"

"Me?" he scoffed. "I never doubted you. Hell, you coulda lit out the first time and never looked back. Anyway, I'm just saying, it was a good thing, you coming back. These people never woulda made it without you leading them. Just wanted to say from the group, thanks."

"Just doing my job, Ervin."

"Bullshit! This is more than that, even if you don't want to admit it. You're a good man." He stood, smiled and moved off.

* * *

Teke stopped her climb on the eighth floor. She wouldn't want to admit it to Stu, but she was too tired to climb any farther. The physical exertion left her drained. Besides, why climb up when everyone else was coming down? She lay on the sofa, staring out the window at the blackness beyond. Her thoughts returned to the moment when she saw Stu outside the bus. Her heart had done flips.

Until then, she'd given serious thought to eating a bullet. She couldn't see any way out. The guilt overwhelmed her and a large tear rolled down her cheek. She wiped at it in anger. She had been so close to quitting. Stu never would've given up. She felt inferior, more so than when he'd moved into the tower and had the attention of all the young elite women. With a sudden spike to her heart, she realized she'd never be good enough for him. The kiss had been stupid. But hadn't he responded? No, not really; not any more than any man, given the thought of getting laid.

She covered her face with both hands as if she could hide from her own foolish notions.

What was that?

She sat bolt upright, her hand reaching for the carbine. Teke turned her head, searching for the sound. It was like a voice. A scrape, like something hitting the wall, brought her to her feet, gun poised, waist-high. Someone was in the outer hallway, and she was pretty sure the crits didn't speak.

She doubted it would be Stu. He would've found some way to announce himself. Although, now that she thought about it, he wouldn't know where she was. It could be other survivors. She had to check. Muscles tensed and nerves steady, but heart rate racing, Teke advanced toward the front door with as much stealth as she could force her body to give.

There, she pressed an ear to wood and focused her hearing. Nothing. She peered through the peephole. The electric was still working; the lights were on. To her surprise, an older man and a tall woman passed by, following a younger man with a gun. They crept with slow, silent progress.

Behind them, a line of men and women followed. None of them had a gun, but almost all wielded a knife or some kind of a weapon. She stepped back and blew out a breath. Her entire body sagged with relief. Deciding to announce her presence, she gripped the door and pulled it open.

"Hey," she whispered. "I'm Corporal— "

Before she could say more, the startled group jumped. Some screamed; others ran, but the man with the gun fired. The bullet struck her high on the right side, slamming her back into the door. Dazed, yet still aware and functioning, she dove back inside the apartment and tried to kick the door shut. One of the men was too fast. He banged the door open and stepped over her. She tried to lift her weapon, but he ripped it from her grasp. Defenseless, the only thing she could think to do was crawl backward.

The gunman entered. A sinister sneer centered on the man's face as he lowered the gun to within inches of Teke's face. She cringed, closed her eyes and tried to speed up her retreat. "Where do you think you're going, little soldier?" He laughed, excited for his kill.

When she didn't feel the bullet, she opened her eyes to see the older man step in behind the shooter and place a restraining hand on the gun. He looked down at Teke and frowned. She recognized him. He was the elite of the elite. The head man, Welsh. He had come to her rescue.

"Don't waste the bullet. We don't have enough as it is."

What? Did she hear him right?

Welsh spoke to someone over his shoulder. "You, Anderson. Go get a pillow and finish her."

Anderson, a tall, fit man, stepped in next to Welsh and looked down at Teke. His face paled at the request. "Why not just leave her? She's going to die here alone anyway."

"Do as I say. Do it now."

"Okay. I don't understand why he shot her, though. Couldn't we use an experienced fighter?"

"Perhaps," said Welsh, "but what's done is done. Besides, once we reach the yachts, we would have had to eliminate her anyway. Get on with it and catch up to us, or we'll leave you behind."

Teke continued to back away, but the loss of blood was making her efforts more difficult. Welsh and the shooter left the room. Anderson watched them go. When he looked back down at Teke, his face was flushed with anger. "Motherfucker better think twice before leaving me behind." He stormed past Teke, heading for the bedroom. "Don't go anywhere, bitch."

As he disappeared through the door, Teke gathered the last remnants of her strength and pushed to her feet. She took short and fast unsteady steps toward the bathroom and lunged through the door just as Anderson was exiting the bedroom, pillow in hands.

He saw her too late. Teke managed to get the door closed

and locked before he could grab her. She leaned her weight against the door as Anderson pounded on it with furious blasts. "Open this fucking door, you stupid bitch whore." The verbal and physical barrage lasted about ten seconds before she heard, "Well, fuck you, then. It's not like you're going to live long, anyway."

Running footfalls faded. Teke slumped to the floor, winced and tried to fight off the paralyzing pain and the tears. She failed and let them come. As a fringe of black circled the edges of her vision, she thought of Stu and that she would never get to kiss him again.

26

Exhaustion-induced sleep had Evan's consciousness drifting. A distant pop registered and his eyes fluttered open. Despite being half asleep, his mind had already tagged the noise as a gunshot. He looked around the room. The collective group was asleep, except for one. His eyes met Jack's. What Evan saw there confirmed his fears.

"Was that a gunshot?" he said.

Evan crawled to him. "You heard it, too?"

"Yeah."

"You weren't sleeping, were you?"

"No. Hell, I've been sleeping so much, I couldn't now if I wanted to."

"You doing all right?"

"Thanks to Little Miss Desiree, I'm doing better." He paused for a second, as if considering something. "That's not a problem, is it?"

In spite of the situation, Evan smiled. "No. It's not a problem at all." Then he returned to the gunshot. "I was half asleep. Where do you think the shot came from?"

"It sounded muffled, like it was inside or from a distance." He shrugged. "I'm not that familiar with gunshots. I don't know."

Evan rolled the information around in his head. His first thought and fear was that the shot came from Teke. He should've checked to see where she was and that she was safe.

"Do you think it's other survivors? Or that it could it be that asshole, Welsh?"

"Either way, it's something I need to check out." He started to rise, but Jack put a firm grip on his forearm. "If it's Welsh ..."

Evan said, "Don't worry. If it's Welsh, he won't be

rejoining the group."

Evan walked over to where Ervin slept and woke the man. "Shh!" He covered the big man's mouth and whispered. "I have to go check something out. I wanted you to know."

"What's going on?"

"I heard a gunshot. I want to know where it came from."

"Welsh?"

"Could be."

"Make sure you say hi from me."

"You got it."

"Be careful."

Evan nodded and went to the balcony. He leaned over and scanned the ground. Radiant light reached out from several floors. Sporadic lighting shone halos on the ground, but nothing that encompassed a large enough area to get a good picture of the grounds. Crits moved in and out of the spotlights, but nothing out of the ordinary moved; the ordinary, which was now the creatures.

He wondered where Teke was. *Only one way to find out.* He lifted his leg over the rail and began the descent once again. At each floor, he stopped and checked the apartments to make sure they were still clear. Nothing had changed until he reached the eighth level. There he found the door open and two crits inside. Someone had been in the room.

Opting for stealth, he dispatched both foes with his knife, then went to the door. To his surprise, he found only four crits patrolling the hall. He closed and locked the door. His peripheral vision caught sight of something on the carpet. He stared at the red splotches, then bent to examine them closer. Someone living had been shot, and recently. The blood was still wet. The scary part was that unless the crits had learned to shoot guns, someone living had shot another living person. He thought of Welsh.

If someone had been shot, there should be a trail. It wasn't hard to find. A long red line led to the hall and to a closed door. He tried the knob. Locked. Standing to the side, he rapped on the door. "Hello? Is anyone in there?"

No response. He tried again. "This is Captain Stewart of the Island Guard. Are you hurt? Do you need assistance?" He pressed the side of his head to the wood. "Teke, is that you?" This time, he pounded, but still got no response. Fear formed a knot in the pit of his stomach. Without knowing why, he had an overwhelming drive to get inside. Turning around, he mule-kicked the door just below the knob. On the second kick, the frame splintered, but something held the door shut.

Evan shouldered the door open until he could poke his head inside. Lying in a pool of blood was Teke. Panic tore through him, his heart threatening to explode. "Teke!" He muscled the door open and dropped next to his friend. Fingers probing, he found a weak pulse. He felt momentary relief, but how long she kept breathing would depend on how quickly he could get help. He knew there was a doctor upstairs who had helped save Jack. But how was he going to get Teke upstairs past all the crits? He couldn't lift her up all those flights. The only solution that came to mind was the elevator. He had to work and move fast.

He tore her shirt open and lifted the layers of undershirts she wore until the wound was exposed. The bullet had entered just below the shoulder. He fingered her back until he found an exit wound. Evan grabbed towels off the racks and pressed them tight against both holes. Holding them in place with one hand, he searched through the cabinet under the sink for anything he could use to stop the blood flow. He found a box of tampons. Using his knife, he cut a towel into strips. Pressing the tampons against the bullet hole on both sides, he tied the strips together and wrapped them around her chest and shoulder. After wrapping several more layers, he pocketed more tampons and ran for the outer door.

With time short, he gave no thought to checking the hall first. Evan burst out the door and carved his way to the elevator. He pressed the call button, then ran to the far end of the hall and closed the fire door. The hall now secure, he raced back for Teke.

Scooping her up, he ran for the hall. The elevator doors

were just closing. Using his foot, he punched the button again and the doors reopened. He set her down and pressed eighteen. What was he going to do when the doors opened and he was faced with numerous crits? He pulled his gun and two extra magazines and waited.

The elevator rose unhindered. His eyes focused hard on the numbers as they passed one by one with agonizing, slow progress. Then came the *ding*. He sucked in and blew out slowly. The doors opened. He stepped out into a horde. The knife and silence would not work now. There were too many and Teke had precious little time for delays. The gun barked over and over.

He kept one foot inside the car to keep the doors open. The bodies piled up quickly. He reloaded once, used his foot to place a body between the doors, then advanced down the hall. He didn't have far to go to get to the room he needed. He kicked, stopped shooting for an instant, and yelled, "Ervin, It's Evan. Open up."

He went back to shooting. Two shots in one direction, two in the other. He was about to kick again when the door opened a crack and Ervin's face stared out. "Quick. In the elevator. I'll cover you."

Ervin hesitated as if not comprehending, then opened the door and ran. Desiree stood at the door staring at him. "Keep it closed, but be ready to open it in a hurry when I call."

The door shut. Evan backed up, firing in alternating directions. Instead of dwindling, the number of crits seemed to be increasing. They were pouring in from the far doorway.

"Okay," Ervin said. "I've got her."

Evan reloaded again and advanced. Ervin stayed close behind, hugging the wall. They reached the door and Evan shouted, "Desiree! Now!"

The door opened and Ervin stepped through. Hands closed in on Evan and he couldn't shoot fast enough. He fired off the remaining rounds in the magazine and ducked inside. He and Desiree attempted to close the door, but several fingers managed to snake through.

"Some of you, come here and help." Two men rushed forward and added their weight to the door. "Hold it in place. Don't give ground." Bracing a knee against the door, Evan drew his knife. As still more fingers wormed their way through the small crack, Evan put his left hand on the spine of the honed blade, and starting at the top, pressed hard, drawing the edge downward and slicing through the dry and brittle bones like they were matchsticks. It took three times before the door would seal.

A hand reached behind him and set the lock. He turned to see Desiree, her face surprisingly calm. "Can some of you drag some of the heavier pieces of furniture over here? I don't think they can get in, but I don't want to take a chance."

The room had come alive with action and the sound of concerned and frightened voices. Evan ignored it all and hurried to where the doctor was examining Teke. He wanted to ask how she was, and more importantly, if she would live, but he refrained, fighting down the words even as the fear pushed them up.

He watched the woman work. She kept muttering in a low voice, the words lost amidst all the commotion. When he saw her shake her head, tears welled. *No!* He couldn't lose Teke. The thought was more than he could take. He spun away and made for the balcony. He covered his face with his hands and struggled to keep the tears in check. *Please, God. Please.*

But, as usual God, was not answering him.

27

The evening dragged on until darkness was but a haze over the horizon. The group stirred from their unsettled sleep, looking only slightly more animated than the crits. Few spoke. Most lay or stood staring off at some unseen visage.

Evan's eyes burned from lack of sleep. He'd been unable to take them off the doctor and her two female assistants, and at the same time, afraid to check on their progress. That they were still working on Teke was both a good and bad thing.

The aroma of coffee drifted through the apartment, stirring memories. He blinked several times as if waking from a dream, and for a moment, felt like he was in a more normal time. A time where the thought of crits was nothing more than an idea for a TV show. He blinked again and the image in his mind dissipated like a popped bubble.

Ervin stood in front of him with a cup of coffee, the steam rising over the rim. Evan pushed himself to a somewhat erect position while his back protested the effort. As he tried to stretch, the rest of his muscles joined in with complaints of their own.

Ervin handed him the cup. The warmth felt good in his hand. So good, he wrapped the other one around it, too.

"Any word?" Ervin asked.

Evan shook his head and sipped the hot beverage. The small taste had a rejuvenating effect. He saw the doctor stand taller, put hands on her lower hips and bend backward. She rotated her neck and exhaled a deep breath. She stepped away from the dining room table she'd been using as an operating table. Her shirt was splattered with blood. Removing the latex kitchen gloves she'd been wearing, she dropped them on a chair. The two women assistants continued to do something over Teke that Evan couldn't see.

He stood watching, afraid to move, the coffee cup pressed

to his lower lip. The smell of the brew no longer registered. His heart raced with an anxiety that blocked out sound and repelled thought. Evan stared, mind blank, as time slowed to a crawl. An eternity had passed by the time the doctor made her way over to him.

In a rush like an explosion of senses, the room came back into focus. The first sound that registered was his own, "Huh?"

The doctor gave a knowing smile, placed a hand on Evan's shoulder and said, "I said, as long as we can keep any infection at bay, she should be fine. I think she cracked her collarbone, but most of the damage is muscular. I did the best I could under the circumstances, but without proper medical equipment, drugs, and personnel, I think we did pretty well. She may lose some mobility in that shoulder, but overall, she was lucky."

Evan swayed. His knees felt weak. He tilted sideways, but Ervin was there to steady him. "Whoa there, Captain. You all right?" He stepped back to avoid Evan's spilled coffee.

"Yeah. Just tired."

The doctor helped Ervin guide Evan to a chair. "Try to drink more than you spill," Ervin said. "I think you're gonna need the jolt."

Evan spoke to the doctor. "Can she be moved?"

She sighed. "Under normal circumstances, I'd say no, but in our current situation," she shrugged. "It's not best, but if we can rig some sort of sling to lower her in a prone position with no stress on the work I just did, we can move her."

"Stu!" Teke's voice shouted over the awakening group's voices. "Stu, don't you let them leave me behind. Get off me."

"Stop that!" one of the nurses said.

Evan handed the coffee to Ervin and hurried to Teke's side. "I'm here, Te-- er, Corporal." She reached out and caught his hand, and yanked him down to her. Her face was a mix of tears and blood. "I'm going with you."

"We're not leaving you."

"You'd better not," she winced.

"Stop moving. Rest for a while so I can figure out how to get you down safely."

"Ahhhh!" she cried out. "Son. Of. A. Bitch."

Evan turned to the doctor who'd come up behind him. "Can we give her something for the pain? We're not gonna be able to move her otherwise."

"All we've got is some ibuprofen." To one of the nurses, she said, "Get her four—no, better make it three—pills. Unless, we find some more, we're going to need to ration them."

"We'll check each apartment on the way down," Evan said.

Ervin shouted over everyone. "Listen up, people. We're going to be heading out in about twenty minutes. Get something to eat, use the bathroom, and do whatever you need to get ready. We want to make an early start so we can get down today."

Everyone began to move in a more motivated fashion. Evan ignored them and lowered closer to Teke. He squeezed her hand tight, then lifted her head so she could swallow the pain pills. She laid back and closed her eyes. He couldn't help but notice how small and fragile she looked. He'd never seen her as anything other than strong and tough. He would've stayed by her side all day if necessary, but Ervin placed a big hand on his shoulder. "We have to get ready, Evan. We have to figure out how to lower her down."

After another squeeze, he released her hand and walked away from the table. "Do we have any extra cable?"

"Yeah, but how do we do this? Rigging up a chair was one thing, but how do we fix something for her to lie down on?"

"We could try a blanket and rig it like a hammock."

Two men and a woman joined them while they brainstormed. The woman, Irene, said, "Can we use a mattress?"

"Too big," Joe, a small, middle-aged man with gray-black hair said.

Irene said, "What if it's a twin-size? That's not too big. We can poke holes through each corner and thread the cable under and up the other side so it hangs like a swing."

"That might work," said Evan. "Is there a twin here?"

"I slept in it last night," Irene said.

"Let's give that a try," said Evan. "Ervin, get people started down. I'll take the cable and rig up the bed. Joe and Irene can help me."

They set about on their tasks. Evan sent Joe to get the cable, while Irene led him to the spare bedroom. He took out his knife and jammed it a few inches inside the end seam. The blade wasn't long enough to puncture the bottom, so he had to turn the mattress over. With a hole in both sides, he pushed the cable through one end, but couldn't fish it through the other. He was forced to carve out a big enough area to allow his hand to slide in and snare the cable.

Pulling it, he wrapped the cable under the mattress to the opposite side where he sliced another hole through the top and bottom. He pushed the cable up and Irene snatched it. They repeated the process on the other end. They each grabbed two ends and lifted. Considering what they had to do, Evan wasn't sure the cumbersome bed would work. "If one person drops an end, she'll fall off."

"What if we strap her to the bed?" Irene offered.

Evan could see the pros and cons. Instead, he took the last piece of cable and tied it around Teke. Joe and Evan lifted her onto the bed and carried her out to the balcony. More than half the group had already made the first climb down. Gathering a small group, Evan explained what he wanted. It took two people to lift Teke and the mattress over the rail, and another four, with one controlling each cable end, to lower her to the next level.

The fear of not being able to see made Teke a threat to herself. She kept leaning to one side to see what was going on. She leaned over too far and threw the balance off. The mattress tipped, and Teke slid off.

28

"Teke!" Evan screamed from above. In an instant, he had one foot perched on the rail, ready to leap to her rescue. She dangled from the lone cable wrapped around her body. "Hold on!" he shouted to the man holding the other end of it. Others leaped into action, grabbing the lifeline. Fortunately, Teke had been lowered far enough that the catchers below could grab her and pull her in.

Evan climbed down and screamed at her. It was difficult to determine who was more frightened by the near fall, Evan or Teke. After getting her to promise she would lie still and trust them, the team of hoisters tried again, this time with much more success. But with Helen, Jack, and now Teke needing special aid, the descent took much longer than he'd hoped.

By midday, they had gone only down six floors. With a dozen yet to go, they took a break for lunch. Evan stood on the balcony, taking in the grounds below. A large mass of crits had formed around both sides of the buses. Many of them stared upward in anticipation of a meal. Their unwavering gazes and deep-set, haunting eyes sent an eerie chill through him.

A shuffling sound drew his attention. He turned as Teke moved next to him. Her wounded arm was tied up and supported against her chest. He smiled. "You should be lying down, resting."

"Don't start with me."

"Stubborn as ever."

"Kiss my ass."

He studied her face, his eyes lingering on her lips. She noticed. "Don't even think about it."

He felt the heat rise to his cheeks and looked away for an instant, then back. "What?"

"Don't play dumb. You know you wanted to kiss me."

The flush flared again.

"And so what if I did? Would that be so bad?"

Her silence made him uneasy. Maybe he shouldn't have said that.

"I thought I lost you. I was, ..."

"Ah, was the big bad captain afraid for me?" she mocked.

He looked away.

Her arm slid through his and she lowered her head to his shoulder. "Well, if you must know, I was pretty damned scared, too."

His body warmed at her touch. He lifted his arm and set it gently around her. "Hey, don't be going all soft on me now, Captain." But she didn't move her head. They stood that way for several moments before she lifted her head. "We should get going again," she said, but as she started to slip away, he turned her to face him, gazed into her eyes, then slowly lowered his lips to hers. A moment's resistance evaporated as their lips touched. Neither one closed their eyes, choosing instead to explore the depths behind them.

Evan still tingled as they broke apart. Their eyes stayed locked together, sharing an even deeper emotional kiss. "Why Captain, is that how you greet all your troops?"

He smiled. "No, just the special ones."

"And do you stand at attention for all the special ones?"

For a moment he was confused, but when the impish grin spread over her face and her eyebrows arched up and down, he understood what she was referring to and turned his body, embarrassed. "No, that's only for the *very* special ones."

She raised on tiptoes and pecked his cheek. "Just don't go saluting anyone else." She walked away without looking back.

Ten minutes later, the first climbers were on their way down again. With each floor they passed, excitement grew until the group became aware of what awaited below. The crowd of undead had grown to at least a hundred. They all seemed to be watching the progress of the descent, swaying with anxious anticipation.

Helen asked, "What are we going to do when we get down there?"

"We'll be fine," Evan said, but in truth, wondered himself.

They reached the ninth floor and were just guiding Helen's chair over the rail, when screams jarred Evan. He looked below in time to see one of the advance climbers fall into the gathered crowd of diners. Immediately, he was lost in their midst as they jammed together to get to him.

Evan took out the gun, leaned over the rail and popped off a series of rounds. He fired in a hurry, not worried about aiming. The horde was too thick to miss. His intent was to clear a path for the fallen man. Finishing one magazine, he ejected, reloaded and fired again. The man screamed, as many on the balconies did likewise.

With the second mag near empty, Evan caught a glimpse of the man's agonized face. He took careful aim and fired twice, wanting to be accurate. Both rounds slammed into the man's face and his screaming stopped. His face disappeared beneath a swarm of grotesque writhing bodies.

Evan continued to watch, his mind shut off to all the sobbing and voices around him. Saddened by the loss and his actions, the weight of guilt bore down upon him. He had no choice; he knew, but it didn't make killing a living person any easier.

Joe leaned over the railing and peered up at Evan. He snapped from his fugue and said, "What happened?"

"He was moving too fast and lost his footing. It happened so quick, none of us had a chance to respond."

The words angered Evan. He shouted, "That didn't have to happen! Take your time. Be safe. No one should climb alone. You all should have a partner. That was an unnecessary and preventable loss, not to mention a waste of almost thirty rounds."

Someone behind him said, "Well, that's pretty cold." He turned to face the woman, whose name he didn't know. She blanched and stepped back. A man put a protective arm around her and said, "Really. You make it sound like the bullets were more important than Ralph was."

Teke rounded on the man. "That's not what he's saying, butt wipe. Ralph is important, but having to use all those bullets to try and save one person means there are less to keep the rest of us safe. And in case you haven't noticed, our descent has drawn a crowd. We're going to need as much firepower as possible by the time we get down there."

No one spoke. The silence became an uncomfortable wedge between Evan and Teke and the rest of the group. "I'll do whatever is necessary to keep you all safe," Evan said. "You have my word. I could've let those animals tear Ralph apart, but if I couldn't save him, I didn't want him to have to live through the agony of having his body devoured. It was the merciful thing to do. I'd expect someone to do that for me, too. I'll do it again if necessary, but please, let's not let that happen again."

Ervin shouted from below. "Are we ready to start again?"

Evan said, "Yes, but make sure you all have a partner."

And with the crits' attention occupied for the moment, the group, minus one person, began its climb again.

29

Ervin joined Evan on the fifth floor balcony. "We've got about an hour's worth of daylight remaining. What do you want to do?"

"I want to push ahead, but I don't want a race between us and the sun. That's how accidents happen and people die. We're close. One more day won't matter."

"So, you just want to see how far we get?"

"I'd like to make it to the third floor. We'll decide what to do from there. If we can reach the second floor, all the better. I want as short as climb as possible for tomorrow. I'd prefer not having to run across the buses in the dark."

Ervin passed the word as the climb continued. Everyone was too weary to make any comment, although some merely grumbled. When they reached the third floor, the sun was but a faint memory. Evan checked the ground below. The area around the tower looked darker than he'd remembered. He looked around and realized the lights had not come on. He watched for a minute, thinking it might still be too early, but then noticed none of the internal lights shone from the first floor windows, either.

He turned and looked into the apartment. Spying Desiree, he said, "Hey Desiree, flick that light switch, would you?" She did, but nothing happened. *Damn!*

"What's that mean?" she asked.

"It means," Joe answered for him, "that without anyone to run the power plant, the electricity is off."

Evan decided it was a good time to call the group together. As the word spread and they huddled in the living room, Evan spoke. "Here's the situation. I'm sure you're all aware by now we no longer have electricity. We need to prepare the food that will go bad in a few days without refrigeration and save what will keep for the journey. I'm not sure how much longer we'll have running water, so everyone should hydrate well tonight and in the morning. I think we'll stop here for tonight. But before the sun is gone completely, I want the advance team to climb down one more flight, then I want to lower Jack, Teke, and Helen. That will save time tomorrow. We should be able to finish early in the morning and be ready to cross the buses."

"Can't we just finish now?" a man said.

"We can, and I'll leave that to a vote, but here's my reasoning. Without light, we risk making more mistakes that could cost more lives. Although the buses are wide enough to walk across, in the dark, one misstep, and someone might fall. If that happens, we might not be able to see well enough to rescue them. I'd rather cross when we can see what we're doing."

A tall, athletic woman said, "What about all those creatures out there?"

"If we take our time and work together, they shouldn't be able to touch us. Once on the other side of the fence, we're home free."

An older woman sobbed.

"I know you're afraid. This has been hard. You've all done well, and look how far we've come. We can do this. Get some food and a lot of sleep."

With no more questions, the team disbursed. Evan went to the balcony to supervise the last climbers. As they readied Helen's chair, Teke walked out. "I'm not going. I'll stay here tonight."

Annoyed, Evan turned to her, but before he could speak, he saw the set of her jaw and the determination in her eyes. She crossed her good arm over the bad one to emphasize her position. Evan sighed. It wasn't worth the fight. "Fine, but go inside, eat, and get to sleep now." He said it in a tone that would've made the others cringe, not sure if it was real or simply to save face with anyone else who'd heard. Teke gave him a mock salute and marched back inside. His anger faded as he watched her until he was left with a wide grin.

When everyone had been lowered, Evan searched out Ervin. The big man had half a sandwich in one hand and a glass of orange juice in the other. He lifted the glass toward Evan as he sat. "Last of the oj. Who knows if we'll ever find any more."

"Enjoy." Evan sat next to him. "We have one problem with the buses that I haven't had a chance to tell you, with everything else that has happened. There's about a four to six-foot-wide gap between the last bus and the fence. Unless we can figure something out, people will have to jump."

Ervin stopped chewing, studying Evan. "That could be a problem. A big problem."

"I don't want to tell the rest yet. They have enough to worry about, but give it some thought."

Ervin nodded. As he sipped his juice, Evan glanced around the room, then leaned closer and whispered. "I'm gonna leave for a while."

The big man stopped drinking. "My room is at the end of the hall. I've got another gun and two more boxes of ammo there. I have a feeling we're gonna need it tomorrow."

"How do you plan on getting there?"

"I've been thinking. I can't risk opening the door. We have no way of knowing what's out there. The best way is to go transverse from one balcony to the next."

"But that's actually farther across than going down. It's only ten feet down, but it must be at least twenty feet across. How do you plan to do this? Swinging like Tarzan?"

"It might be the best way, but not the safest way. I'm going to climb down, run along the buses until I've got enough space away from the crits to jump down, then I'll run to the balcony beneath mine and climb up."

"You say that as if it's the easiest thing in the world to do."

"Piece of cake."

"Yeah? And what if you fail? Then we're left with no leader and no gun."

"I've thought about that, too. Since the objective is to avoid any trouble, I'll leave the gun with you. You're also more than capable of taking over leadership, especially this close to the end."

Ervin gazed hard at Evan, then said, "Man."

"Hey, it's the only way to do it."

"You sure we need the gun that bad that it's worth the risk?"

"Wouldn't you feel better about descending into that mob with more firepower?"

"How will you get back?"

"Yeah, that part is the trickiest."

"They seem to be much more aware than I remember. They'll be waiting for you."

"But on the way back, I'll have the gun."

Ervin shook his head. "I don't like it. It's not worth risking your life."

"And yet, I'm going anyway."

"Of course you are. Because there's just not enough excitement for you now."

Evan smiled. "Wish me luck." He offered his hand.

"Luck." The big man squeezed Evan's to a point that he feared Ervin might not let go. Then the grip eased and he retracted his hand. "You better come back, or that girl of yours might decide to take it out on me."

"I'm going to give her a chance to get to sleep before I go. The fewer people who know, the better."

He stood, took off his holster and the pouch on his belt that held the extra ammo, and handed them to Ervin. He took them, but Evan's hand refused to let go as if it had a mind of its own. Then he opened his hand and turned away, hoping he hadn't made a huge mistake.

30

Evan waited two hours, giving his group a chance to settle in for the night. He had six people below and twenty-three, not counting himself, up here. With as much stealth as possible in the crowded space, he worked his way to the balcony. The cables were all attached, ready for the morning's climb. He stepped over the balcony, about to drop and hang, when he heard, "I knew you were up to something stupid when I saw you huddling with Ervin."

The voice shocked him off balance and almost off the ledge. Teke stood there, arms crossed again.

"I'm just going to check on the people below."

"Don't bullshit me. At least have the courtesy to tell me the truth." She came closer, squatted and peered at him through the bars.

"I'm sorry. I'm going to get another gun."

She nodded. "And you know where one is? Close?"

"Yes."

"Then why sneak away?"

He tried to form an answer, but knew she'd see through another lie. She answered for him. "Because it's in a place that it's dangerous to get to, right?"

He swallowed hard, like a kid caught by a parent doing something he shouldn't. He sighed and nodded.

To his surprise, she stood, looked down at him, and said, "Be careful." Then she turned and walked back inside.

He hung by the rail for a moment, replaying the last moment before deciding nothing had changed. Extending his arms and then his legs, he reached the second floor balcony. Without pausing, he continued down to the first floor. As his feet touched the railing, hands clutched at his legs. He jumped to the balcony in a hurry, his heart thudding hard against his chest. He hadn't thought about being within arm's reach of the creatures. He would have to let the group know before they climbed down in the morning to make the last descent over the center rail to avoid being dragged down.

He squatted and listened as the creatures stretched their arms through the spindles, trying to get to him. He prayed the bars would hold. If not, his group would be stranded. Taking a few deep breaths to calm his nerves, he stepped forward, placed his hands on the front rail and vaulted over it. His feet landed on the sloped top of the windshield. His feet began to slide downward. The bus rocked as the bodies pressed against it from both sides.

Placing his feet against the wipers, he pushed up to the roof. He waited in a squat for a heartbeat before attempting to cross. As he became more sure of his footing, he picked up speed. Reaching the place where the second and third buses' noses came together, he ran down the windshield and leaped. His feet touched the ground and he went into a squat and roll, coming up running. By his second stride, the knife was in his hand.

Though he couldn't see well, he felt he had a slight lead. He ran straight along the street, trying to draw as many away from the building as possible. He was upon a crit before he could react. Dodging to the side, he swiped with his knife, but didn't have enough room to avoid the collision. At the speed he ran, the blow was enough to throw him off balance and to the ground.

His knee and hip hit the street hard. He absorbed the pain as best he could, relegating it to the back of his thoughts and scrambled to his feet. He couldn't continue in the dark. Reaching behind him, he pulled a small flashlight from his back pocket. He flicked it on, scanned the area to get his bearings, and switched it off.

The brief illumination showed him he did have space to move, but not as much as he'd hoped. He raced forward, flicking the beam on and off every few seconds. When a crit got too close, he flashed the light in the creature's eyes, giving himself a moment to either get past or cut it down.

When he arrived at a spot even with the balcony he was looking for, he swerved and ran toward the building.

The crits pursuing him from where he'd climbed down from had a better angle at him now, so he increased his speed to an all-out run. Almost too late, he flicked on the light and avoided racing directly into the cement platform and iron bars. He skidded to a halt and slid on the grass, his legs extending under the platform.

He righted himself without looking back. He didn't want to know how close his pursuers were. Besides, to look would only slow him down. Reaching for the bars, he lifted his foot and placed it on the ledge. He managed to get one leg over before several hands found his other leg and latched on. He kicked hard, but to no avail. Their grips were surprisingly strong, digging into his flesh, igniting more desperate kicking. He reached over and slashed wildly with the knife. The blade bit and carved, but more hands gripped him. His weight shifted as the pull increased. Panic rose within him. His arms and legs thrashed in frantic unison. From a close, unknown source, a whimpering reached his ears.

So far, he didn't think any of the attempted bites had penetrated his pants. He drove the knife straight down into a crit's head, but the blade hit at a poor angle and skidded off. Bracing his foot against the inside of the railing, he pushed hard for leverage while pulling his body upward. He could gain no ground, other to delay the inevitable.

Snarling a combat yell, he threw himself at them in one last fury of slashes and kicks, this time aimed at their arms rather than at their heads. He was unaware of the presence behind him until the gun blasted near his ear. He twisted to see a young girl of about twelve holding a gun with both hands. She fired one round after another until the gun emptied. Her efforts were just enough to lessen the force against him.

With one violent kick, he freed his leg and fell backward over the rail. His body caught the girl and dragged her down with him. Still panicked at his near miss, he grabbed the girl, lifted her and darted for the safety of the apartment. He fell to the floor and released her. The two rolled to a stop facing each other.

Her face was tear-streaked. Evan wondered about his own face. As a sudden afterthought, he crawled to the sliding door, closed and locked it, then collapsed on his back gaze unfocused as he stared at the ceiling. Beside him, the young girl cried softly. Neither spoke for several long minutes until she broke the silence. "Are-are you all right?"

He turned to look at her. "Yes, thanks to you. You saved me." He sat up and lifted his pant legs and examined the skin. In the dark, he could feel no evidence of puncture wounds or blood or that the skin had been broken. Relieved, he flopped back down.

"I-I was afraid."

"Yeah; me, too."

"No. I mean I was afraid of you."

That surprised him. "Why? Did you think I would hurt you?"

"Yes, like the men who took my mom. She screamed and-and fought, but they hit her and dragged her away."

"Why didn't they take you?"

"When the apartment door crashed open, we were in the bedroom. She told me to hide under the bed and no matter what I heard or saw, not to come out." She cried harder and Evan sat up. "I don't understand. I thought the crits were the enemy. Why would they take her?"

Evan thought of one reason; the most basic of reasons, but even in the most desperate of times, man has proven his ability to sink ever lower. Then, a new thought came to mind. "How long ago was this?"

"Last night."

"How many men?"

"Three. All older. I think there might have been a woman, too. One of them had a gun. I should've tried to get to the gun my mom had hidden under the pillows, but she told me to stay. Since they were alive, she didn't think they were a threat. She thought we'd been rescued. Then they hit her, and the one guy said he would do terrible things to her if she didn't cooperate and go with them. Where were they going? Why were they so mean?"

Evan had a sinking feeling he knew who her captors were. Welsh and his posse. But what would they want with the woman? They had already shown they didn't want any more people in their group. He was sure they planned to use her in some fashion, but other than in the obvious sexual way, what other purpose could she serve? Then it came to him, and his heart sank. She would be the decoy, used as live bait to lead the crits away while Welsh's party made a break for the yachts. That meant they were close. If he didn't stop them, his own group's escape would be in jeopardy. He had to reach his gun.

31

Teke refused to watch Stu go. Her nerves would be on end as it was, and watching him climb down and try to evade that pack of animals would only make things worse. Besides, with no lights shining, following his path would be difficult, leaving his fate to her vivid imagination. No, it was better this way, just to believe he made it.

She settled down and closed her eyes, but she knew sleep would not come to her. Still, she had to try. Her arm ached, making it difficult to find a comfortable position. After several wasted minutes, she stood and went to find something to drink. The remnants of a pot of tea sat on the counter. Though the electricity was gone, they'd been fortunate to still find water in the lines. How much longer that would last, they couldn't know, but Jack had been the one to suggest they not waste what little they might have on washing up or brushing teeth, and flushing the toilet should be reserved for "number twos."

Fishing out the bottle of ibuprofen from her pocket, she swallowed two. They wouldn't do much more than take the edge off, but that was better than nothing. The doctor had stripped the bandage, examined the wound and redressed it. "Looks good so far," she had said. "No sign of infection. Let's keep our fingers crossed." She smiled and tried to look optimistic, but Teke read the concern in her eyes.

She feared the worst. If infection set in, they had little in the way of medical supplies to treat it. It would spread, and eventually she would have to make the decision to either lose her arm or her life. She had already decided it would be her life. She could not, would not, go through whatever was left of her life with only one arm. How long could she survive, anyway?

And what about Evan? He wouldn't want to be with her if

she only had one arm. He respected her now because of her toughness. How tough could a one-armed person be in this world? No, her decision was made. When no one was around to stop her, she would eat a bullet. The thought of it buckled her knees. She clutched at the counter to keep from falling, but the action sent a blinding spike of pain from her shoulder through her entire body.

Lowering her head to the counter, she gritted her teeth. Strangely, the sharpness of the pain seemed to buoy her. She waited, unwilling to move until she had control of her body. Teke offered up a prayer, but afraid she might be limited in that regard, she chose to say it for Stu instead of for herself.

"Please, God—" A flurry of gunshots sounded from below. She bolted upright, ignoring the new blast of pain and hobbled to the balcony. Others were. She pushed her way to the front. "What's happening? Can anyone tell?"

A man spoke. "Someone is shooting from that first floor balcony." He pointed, but she could not see what his arm extended toward. "I could only see the muzzle flash, but I think it was Evan, and I think it was the first balcony next to the lobby."

That sounded right. His room was the first one on the third floor. That was the row of balconies he would've climbed. Since he was shooting and Ervin had the gun, that must mean he'd reached his room and was already coming back. "Could you see what he was shooting at?" She adjusted her statement. "I mean, could you tell if they were crits or humans?"

"I think it was crits, and from the brief look I got, I think there's a lot of them."

Teke's heart sank with a heavy thud. Her body began to slump. Before she realized what was happening, multiple hands grabbed and lifted her. For a brief second, she feared they would toss her over the rail. Instead, they carried her inside and placed her on a couch. Through a misty haze, she saw the doctor leaning over her. She touched Teke's forehead and winced as if she had been burned. "Damn! She's got a fever."

Then her eyes closed and darkness swallowed her.

* * *

"What's your name?" he asked his savior.

"Melody," she said through her tears. "My mom's name is Joan. Can you save her? Please."

He didn't know how to answer. He didn't want to lie to her, but the truth might be too much for her in her emotionally fragile condition. "I don't know. I'll try. I promise, but I don't know where they took her," he said, although he did have an idea. "Can I see the gun?"

Melody looked from the gun to him, then back to the gun, as if trying to decide if she could trust him. Making the choice, she pushed the weapon across to him. Evan picked it up. It was a revolver and it was empty. "Did your mom have any more bullets for this?"

"I don't know." She shrugged. "If she did, they'd be in the bedroom." She pointed down the hall.

Evan stood. "Come on. Show me."

Melody stood and led the way. She opened the door but did not enter. Evan walked past her into the room. The mattress was half off the bed. A lamp had fallen from the nightstand and lay broken on the carpet. He turned to her. "Where did she keep the gun?"

"In the nightstand."

Evan placed the flashlight in his teeth, pulled the drawer open, and rifled through the contents. He found one bullet loose, near the back. He grabbed it, then searched with more energy. Finally, too frustrated with having to move everything, he yanked the drawer out and upended it on the floor. An assortment of items scattered, but the carpet held them close. Evan combed through them, finding three more bullets. A further search of the room came up empty.

Disappointed, he loaded the gun. Four bullets were better than none. He stood. Something crunched under his foot. He bent to examine what it was. A plastic pharmacy pill bottle lay cracked, its capsules spread on the carpet. Evan started to walk away, but something occurred to him and he backtracked. Picking up the broken bottle, he read the label. Amoxicillin. He thought about Teke and Jack and wondered if these antibiotics would help them. "Are these yours?"

"No, my mom's. She had a sinus infection."

Evan dropped to his knees and began scooping up the pills. "Find me something to put them in. Another pill container, or a baggie or something." Melody disappeared. While he gathered the pills and tried to salvage the broken ones, Evan heard her rummaging in the dark kitchen. She returned a minute later with a clear baggie. He dumped the pills into the bag and shoved it into his pocket.

Back in the front room, Evan flashed the light on Melody for a moment. She blinked and lifted a hand to block the light. It was time to go, but how to tell her? He formed and reformed the words in his mind. They sounded right. She was a brave young woman. She would understand. "Melody. I need you to listen to me for a minute. I have to go somewhere, but you can't go with me."

Before he could explain further, the brave young woman went ballistic, going from a berserker attack to a full-blown meltdown. He'd certainly misjudged that.

32

Evan fought her for fifteen long minutes. In many ways, the battle was more intense and more physically and emotionally draining than facing a hallway full of crits. When he finally calmed her enough to be able to listen, he explained again.

"I'm only going two floors up. I can't take you with me. I only have four bullets to defend with, so I'm going to have to move fast. You will not be able to keep up with me and If I have to keep looking back for you, it will put us both in danger."

"You've got what you want and you're going to leave me. You're no better than the men who took my mom." The mention of her mother brought a new intensity to her. "Mom!" She wailed. "You promised!" she shrieked, the pitch so high it made him cringe. "You promised you would rescue my mom!" She launched at Evan and flailed anew.

He caught her arms, but not before she got in a few shots. Perhaps motivated by her fury, Melody was stronger than she looked.

"Melody. Listen." His voice rose, trying to out-yell her. "I'm coming back. I have to come this way to get back to my friends."

"No. You're going to leave me. I know you are."

Evan had no idea how to handle the girl. Even with her hands secured, she kicked him in the shin so hard, he thought she might have broken the bone. He hopped on one foot and tried to keep back from her. Unable to deal with her anymore, he gave her a hard shove. She flew backward, flipping over a chair and landing hard on the floor.

She sprawled, not moving, except for her sobbing. Guilt punched him as he feared he'd hurt her. *Damn it! What was he going to do with her?* He flopped on the couch and rubbed his shin. This was taking too much time.

He looked at the TV and made up his mind. Standing he walked to the TV and pushed it aside. Finding the old cable outlet from the days when it still existed, he drove his knife into the wall above it. Using both hands, he pulled the blade up and sliced through the drywall. Making a parallel line about three inches away from it, he pried a section out, then began ripping with his hands.

Melody sat up and watched, but said nothing. At least her sobbing—and more importantly, her attacks—had stopped.

Latching on to the cable, he pulled it upward. The cord tore a jagged path through the wall. When it reached the ceiling, Evan could rip no more. He had a little more than eight feet of cable, not nearly enough, but it would have to do.

He turned to Melody. His voice hard, he said, "All right, girlie. You wanted to go, now you're going."

Whatever she saw in his face scared her. She screamed and backed away. "What are you going to do? You're going to tie me up, aren't you?"

He paused for a second. He hadn't thought about that option. It would be safer for her if he did. He remembered the kick and her attempts to rake his eyes with her nails. It might be safer for her, but not for him.

Anger flared and he shouted. "You want to go, this is the only way you can. If you don't like it, then you're staying. I don't have any more time to waste on you. A lot of people are relying on me to return to them. I will not leave you behind, but if you insist on going with me, then you need to listen. Otherwise, I'm out of here."

"What do you want me to do? What's the cable for?"

She was still wasting time by asking too many questions, but at least she wasn't shrieking anymore.

"I don't think we can get to my room by going out the door. The only other option is to climb up. I can do it on my own, but you're too short. You will need my help. I'm going to tie this under your arms and hoist you to the next balcony.

You understand?"

She nodded, but with her understanding came fear as she recognized exactly what she would face. "You mean we have to go out there and try to climb with those-those things grabbing at us?"

"Now you're starting to catch on. That's why I wanted to leave you here and pick you up on the way back. It's safer for both of us."

"No." Her eyes began to leak again. "I won't stay here alone. Something might happen to you and I'll be waiting here, never knowing."

"If something happens to me and you're with me, then something will happen to you, too. Don't you get it? Whether or not I come back, this is still the safest place for you."

"But for how long? How long will my food and water last? The electricity is already off. If you don't come back, I'm going to have to go out and face them alone. If I'm going to die, I'd rather it be with you. At least then, I have a chance."

Evan sighed. "Okay, let's do this. But don't you fight me or argue with me on anything. You do exactly as I say, or I swear, I'll leave you behind."

"No, you won't."

"Why? 'Cause you think I'm a nice guy?"

"No, 'cause I'll hurt you if you do."

Evan grunted, not doubting those words for an instant.

He wrapped the cable around her and tied the ends tight. He wanted to do a double wrap, but the cable was already too short. He only had six feet to work with now and a ten-foot distance to cover. Taking in her height of about five feet minus perhaps a foot and a half where the cable was tied, but losing the rest of her height by having to go over the railing above, the length was going to be tight. The best way to make it work was to have her stand on the rail, but with all the hands reaching for her, one slip, and she would be dead.

Evan looked up, trying to best judge how to get over the rail while keeping hold of the cable. No matter how he figured it, the length was not going to reach. He needed something else. He found it in the bedroom. Using his knife, he cut the rope cord on the window blinds and got another three feet to work with. He would not be able to lift her with the cord, but if he tied it to the end of the cable, he would be able to climb with it attached to his belt, then pull the cord until the cable was in reach.

Securing the line, he placed a hand on each of Melody's shoulders. "Are you sure you want to do this?"

She nodded, but her expression said she wasn't sure at all.

"Remember, don't panic. Grab this knot here with both hands in case it starts to slip. It shouldn't, but I'd rather you be prepared. If I need you to step up on the rail, do it fast. Use one hand to balance against the wall and hold the knot with the other. At no time raise your arms over your head. The cable will slip right off. You got all this?"

She nodded. He saw her swallow hard. "It's not too late to change your mind." She shook her head.

She was brave, he'd give her that. Perhaps not too smart, but he couldn't deny her courage. He grabbed her face in both hands and planted a kiss on her forehead.

"What was that for?"

"Luck."

"Oh! Good. Now that you have me all tied up, for a moment, I thought you were gonna go all perv on me."

33

He slid the door open as quietly as possible. The smell of rotted, putrefied flesh wafted into the room. *There must be a lot of them out there for the odor to be this strong.* A strange buzzing began increasing in intensity, like a crowd of paparazzi coming to life when the celebrity they'd been stalking finally made an appearance.

Nails that had grown long after death scraped against the metal spindles, sending an eerie chill up his spine. Evan set a chair down a foot away from the rail to make it easy for Melody to step to the top. Melody, however, balked at exiting the room. Evan tugged on the cable, but she resisted. It was better for her to find out now that she didn't want to climb up, rather than when her feet were being snatched at.

"It's okay. I'll be back in a few minutes." He dropped the cable, stepped to the rail and placed a foot on top.

"No!" Melody screamed and rushed forward, wrapping her arms around his waist. The force of the contact almost pushed him off the rail into the crits. They surged forward, sensing the closeness of their next meal.

Evan jumped back, his heart pounding so fast and hard that he feared it might explode. "What the hell are you doing? You could've killed me. See? This is what I was afraid of. It's better for you to stay here."

She squeezed tight and he returned the embrace with equal ferocity. The close call had him edgy now. As they stood there, he began to wonder how smart his own plan was. With so many crits waiting for them, how would he get down from there? He might have to rethink his escape route. But regardless of what he decided, now that he'd come this far, he still needed that gun.

He grabbed her shoulders and pushed her away, giving an unnecessary violent jerk at the end. "Last chance. Go or stay.

I can't wait for you."

Setting her resolve, she said, "I'm going."

"Then let's do this. No more hesitation. No more panic."

Evan picked up the cord and tied it to his belt. "Wait for me to tell you to get on the rail." Without waiting for a reply, Evan stepped onto the rail, balanced, and reached for the spindles above. His fingers gripped them as hands found his legs. One of the beasts already had teeth pressing into him. He kicked once and swung clear of the rail. Bending his knees, he placed his feet flat against the outer wall. Pulling with his arms, he walked the exterior until he was parallel to the upper platform.

Sliding an arm through the spindles for support, he got his body up high enough to rest his knee on the narrow ledge outside the rail. From there, the climb was easy. He pulled to the top bar and stood, then lifted his legs over and was done. Taking a moment to catch his breath, he leaned on the rail and tried to see the balcony connected to the room where he'd left Teke and the group. He thought about flicking the flashlight on, but decided against it.

For a second, he contemplated climbing on without pulling Melody up, but he feared the girl would panic and try to climb up on the rail herself. He untied the rope, but waited a beat before telling Melody to climb up. He wanted to make sure he was rested enough for the effort he was about to exert. "Can you hear me?"

"Y-yes."

"I'm going to pull the cord so I can grab the cable. Stand on the chair. Get ready." Though the rope was long enough to go over the top of the rail, the cable was not. Evan had to get on his knees and reach through the bars to get a hold of it. He would not have the leverage from that position to lift Melody. She would have to stand on the rail. But that meant she would be there for a second or two while he transferred the cable over the top rail. There was no other way.

"Okay, Melody. Stand on the rail. Now!"

The cable slacked. She screamed and the cable was jerked

from his hands. Panic rushed through him. His lungs exploded their load with no new supply available. Visions of Melody being carried away and born down raced through his mind. Evan lunged at the cord and snagged it, but the grip was tenuous. He looped a length around two fingers and pulled to draw it taut. She was still attached. "Melody!"

The cord pulled hard, yanking his arms downward. He couldn't see, but didn't dare risk letting go with one hand to pull out the flashlight. Another scream. "Melody. Answer me." No response. He fought the line like he was trying to land a swordfish. He leaned over the rail as far as he dared. The cord slacked, then tightened again.

"Damn it, girl, answer me."

"I'm okay," she said finally. "They grabbed me and I got scared. Sorry."

"This isn't working, Melody. You stay there. I'll be back in a few minutes."

She screamed again, this time with more volume and chilling fear. "They're climbing up! Oh my God, they're getting on the balcony!"

Shit! He leaned back and began tugging. "Get on the railing. Hurry!" The rope slacked. Hand over hand, he drew the cord up.

"Hurry!" she shouted.

His fingers touched the cable. He latched on and put every ounce of strength into his pull. By the amount of resistance he felt, he knew she was in the air. He could not see her, but reached forward to grab another length. The cable slipped and Melody screamed again.

Evan hit the bar just below his rib cage with such force, he feared it would break away from its wall anchors. This time, he made a circle with his hand as he pulled, wrapping the cable around his fist. He did it again and a third time, and Melody's head came into view.

His arms burning from the strain, Evan let out a shout, like a weightlifter reaching for that last burst of strength, and pulled again. Melody reached for the spindles and pulled her body toward them. While Evan maintained her height, she lifted a leg and slid it onto the ledge. With the weight slackened, Evan drew the cable in as far as it would go, then sat down to keep it taut. Melody stood and climbed over the rail, falling to the platform. The only sound was the harsh blasting of their lungs fighting for air.

When at last she could speak, Melody said between gulps of air, "Okay—for the record—you were right. I should've— stayed there."

Though he was dying to say, "I told you so," he couldn't draw in enough air to get the words out. He closed his eyes and tried to think of a better way to get Melody to the next floor.

34

When he finally decided to get up and open the door a crack, it took less than a second to determine the hall was impassable. He shut and locked it before he was noticed. That settled it. There was only one way up. But then, something dawned on him. *Shit!* He forgotten that he'd opened the door and let the crits in his room. He might not be able to get into his apartment.

"We have a problem," he said. She sat up and stared at him. "When I left my room, I let the crits in to distract them. I think I shut the door on the way out, but I'm sure there will still be quite a few in my room. I can't take you with me."

Anger flashed through her eyes and a look of betrayal covered her face. "You liar. You're trying to leave me behind."

His own anger flared, unchecked. He rushed forward, shoving her back and straddling her. His hands pinned her shoulders to the floor, rage replacing the emotions had shone before. "That's enough. I'm trying to protect you. I am not lying about what's up there, and I will not take you with me. You're just gonna have to trust that I'll come back for you. I'm sick of you arguing with me. It is not safe. Can you get that through your head?'"

He froze then, his own fear turning his blood to ice. Without realizing it, he'd been banging her head on the floor as he spoke. How many times had he done it? His anger had been so blinding, he had no recollection of doing it at all. "Melody?" He released her and pressed a finger to her carotid artery. The pulse was strong. "Melody!" He patted her face. She groaned. When she opened her eyes, they went wide with terror. "Oh God, Melody. I'm sorry. I didn't mean to hurt you."

She covered her face and wept. "Get off me," she said, her

voice strained. He pulled away and stared at her, horrified by his actions. He lifted his hands and stared at them as if they had acted of their own free will. Even pulled his knees to his chest and rested his head on them. A pounding pressure built within, making thought more difficult.

Melody crawled away, still whimpering. "You're just as bad as the men who took my mom. I hate you. Go! Leave me. I'll be better off."

He had no idea how to fix what he'd done. "Melody, I'm sorry," he said again.

"I don't care. I hate you. You're a liar and-and, ..." She couldn't find further words to describe him.

He stood. Maybe it was for the best. At least now, she would stay. The only way for him to make up for what he'd done was to come back and get her to the group. She could hate him all she wanted then; she'd be safe.

"I'll be back for you."

"I don't care if you ever come back. I hope the crits eat you."

Without another word, he walked out of the room and scaled the rail. He lifted his head above the platform and to his relief, saw that he had closed the sliding door. The balcony was safe; however, the front room was full of creatures. He finished his climb and stood to the side of the glass door. Peering in, he tried to get a head count, but since it was dark, it wasn't possible. He guessed at a dozen, but he had no idea how many more were in the bedroom. That door stood open, just as he'd left it. From his position, he couldn't tell if the front door was closed He had no idea what he'd be dealing with once he made it inside.

He watched the movement by the sliding door, trying to get a feel for when to make his move. The best scenario would be for him to get into the bedroom and close the door without having to expend his bullets. Then he could deal with things, knowing no more would come in. He figured he had about a fifty-fifty chance. Once in the room, though, the odds dropped drastically.

Evan leaned over the rail, trying to find an angle to see into his bedroom, but it was too dark. He would be going in blind. The thought sent a shiver up his spine. He looked down at the gun and the knife and wondered if he might be facing his last battle. Walking away was the best option. He paused, taking in everything that mattered at the moment. The group, escape, Melody, Teke, Welsh. *Welsh!* Evan thought. The name left a bad taste in his mouth. The man had to pay for what he'd done. His actions were criminal and he would not get away with it. Angered now, he looked again at the gun. No, for what he had yet to do, he needed more firepower. Fueled by the goal of getting his people to safety, as well as finding Welsh and taking his revenge, Evan reached for the handle.

He sucked in two large breaths, flicked on the flashlight and placed it between his teeth, then yanked the sliding door open. As soon as he stepped in, the crits reacted to the light. In a flurry of motion, attacking them before they could react, he strode through the horde, slashing and stabbing with the knife and bludgeoning with the butt of the handgun.

Bodies slumped and crumbled around him as he cleared a path to the bedroom. So fast and furious was his assault, that not one of them laid a hand on him. Reaching the door, he slammed a kick in to the chest of a male who blocked his entry, sending him flying backward into several others. The *snap* of a brittle bone was audible.

He slammed the door before any others could enter from the front room. The light reflected back off the sunken and hideous eyeballs of ten crits. Having gained access to the room, Evan wasn't as hesitant about using his four bullets. He stabbed, driving the knife into an eye socket, the blade scraping against bone. He pulled it free and placed the barrel of the gun against the forehead of a woman creature, and pulled the trigger. Skull fragments flew across the room as the body was blown back.

Evan slashed off a hand as it touched his arm, kicking the creature away, and buried the knife in the side of another skull. He fired his second round, dropping another then turned the knife on two crit women. The third shot blasted a short undead man off his feet. Evan decided to save the last bullet for an emergency.

His arm was getting weary from the slashing and thrusting. His mouth had gone dry from breathing through it. His jaw ached as he tried to keep the light in place. He tried to sidestep toward the dresser where his backup gun and ammo were, but the remaining crits blocked his way. He was having a hard time trying to see where to step, as the undead he'd kicked to the ground were crawling toward him. He felt them more than saw them begin to close in around him. Panic increased his heart rate and formed an uncomfortable vise across his chest.

With a new release of adrenaline, Evan went berserk, swinging, kicking, stabbing, and screaming like a Viking warrior. A sudden pain in his leg terrified him and he opened his mouth, losing the flashlight. Fearing his skin had been broken by a bite, he envisioned himself infected with the same disease that had created these monsters. How much time did he have?

He pressed the barrel against the creature on the floor and fired off his last round, wondering if maybe he should have saved it for himself. A millisecond montage of the people he would disappoint flashed before his eyes. He was becoming emotional; his attacks were weak and sloppy. He missed two strikes in a row. Fingers scraped at him from all sides. Their pungent, decaying bodies pressed in tighter. His cheeks were moist with sweat and tears.

He backed away until he hit the wall. He drove one back with the knife and stomped on another crawler. He couldn't tell how many more were left. The cone of light from the fallen flashlight was aimed at the back wall. Shapes and shadows came for him like something from a child's worst nightmare.

Dread encompassed him, announcing to his brain that the end was near. He stabbed forward, the blade finding its mark.

As he withdrew the knife, the back of his hand smacked the dresser next to him. The pain replaced his fear, allowing an idea to penetrate. Grabbing the tall five-drawer chest, Evan shoved it away from the wall and slid behind it.

The wooden piece had some weight to it, but fueled by the notion that this might be his last chance, Evan muscled it forward, pushing the creatures back. Knowing the move had only bought him perhaps a minute's reprieve, he swept his knife hand in an arc to clear space, then turned the dresser with the drawers facing him. He walked it backwards until he was trapped in a corner. Then he tugged on the drawer that held the gun. His own cleverness had now worked against him. The wall blocked the drawer from opening. Feeling the panic rise once more, he screamed and shoved one side away. The open space made him vulnerable, but he was able to pull the drawer open enough to slide his hand inside.

A hand snaked around the dresser and slapped at his head. He flashed the blade upward, severing a finger, but still the hand searched for him. He smacked it away while his other hand patted the inside of the drawer for his gun. "Where is it?" he shouted. Other More hands now made their way around the other end. He was running out of time. *This couldn't be happening.* On the verge of breaking down into a blubbering emotional lump on the floor, Evan sniffled and made a weak stab with the knife as if it no longer mattered. The end was a given.

Then, one of the crits kicked the flashlight, and like an angelic light from above, the cone of light arced his way just far enough for him to see he was searching in the wrong drawer. With new hope, he slammed the drawer shut and tore open the one below it.

Cold fingers touched his neck and walked their way down his back. Evan cried out, spun and grabbed the arm. He shoved it back, then embedded the knife through both arm and wall, pinning it in place. He ducked and returned to his task. Desperate fingers probed and found the box of bullets. The angle was bad. He needed just a bit more space to open the drawer farther. Using his foot, he inched the dresser back a bit. It wobbled, threatening to topple over. Evan had little time remaining.

He slid his arm into the drawer and scooped the contents forward. He could now see the gun. He snatched it up, chambered a round, and just as the dresser fell away, he stood and fired. Sweeping from left to right, Evan pulled the trigger in a steady cadence. One by one, the remaining creatures fell away, no longer a threat.

When no crits were left standing, Evan leaned forward, placing his hands on his knees, and began cackling like a crazed maniac. Unable to stop as his mind retreated to a hidden recess in his brain, he lost track of all thought and time. Then he vomited, though with little in his stomach, it quickly turned to uncontrollable retching.

A noise next to him snapped him back to reality. He stood and turned toward the sound. The crit he had pinned to the wall was still trying to reach him. With a ferocity he thought he was incapable of, he battered the creature's skull with the butt of the gun until nothing remained above its neck. The body hung by the knife.

Evan stood staring at the damage, trying to draw breath where no air seemed to exist. His chest heaved; his arms hung heavy. For a long while, he was unable to move. So tired. He just wanted to move to the bed and lie down. Then he remembered the people were still counting on him. He reached up, grabbed the knife handle, and with great effort, pulled it from the wall. The body slid off the blade and to the floor.

As he bent to retrieve the flashlight, a hand came out as if shot from the darkness outside into the cone of light and wrapped around his wrist. Startled, Evan let out a shout and fired more rounds than were necessary into the creature. He leaned back against the wall for a few minutes, then pulled the drawer out of the fallen dresser and laid it on the bed.

He found the two boxes of ammo and reloaded the magazine. Placing the boxes in his pockets, he walked to the door and stood facing it. He thought about checking his leg where the creature had bitten him, but he didn't want to know. Not yet. The battle was not over and he had to get his people—all of them—to safety first. And he still had to find and deal with Welsh. Even if he were now infected, he should have time enough to finish what he started, but he didn't want to think about that. Once the mission was completed, he'd go off on his own to take care of himself before he changed.

He thought of Teke and was overcome by sadness. His eyes blurred. *No!* He didn't have time for any more emotional behavior. He put his game face back on and reached for the bedroom doorknob.

35

Ten minutes later, he stood on the balcony of his apartment and stared out into the darkness. The battle in the front room hadn't taken long at all. It was amazing what a difference having a gun made. He had mowed them down like dried weeds.

Now as he stood there, he remembered how only a few days ago he had stood in this same place and marveled at the view. He wondered if he had made the right decision by accepting the invitation to move into the tower. That had seemed so long ago now. So much had changed.

He wondered, too, how many of the residents had gotten off the island. Where would they go from here? And would he ever know whether they did or not? He hoped as many of them as possible had stayed together. It was safer that way.

Evan looked down. The distance to the ground seemed so far away. He wasn't sure he had the strength to make the climb. An image of Melody came to mind. For her sake, he had to scale down at least one level. He'd promised, and God knew he had much to make up to her.

He turned to look one last time into the apartment. His eyes came to rest on the refrigerator. He smiled, knowing what lay within. Evan walked through the mounds of rotted and destroyed body parts and opened the refrigerator door. The light didn't come on, but he knew where he was reaching. As his hand wrapped around the bottle neck, he was happy to find a chill still remained.

He twisted the cap of the beer and drank deeply. Beer, wine, or any type of alcoholic beverage was like gold. It wasn't often that his team came across the items anymore while on patrol. Most of what they found went to the elites in the tower, but some made its way to the residents, who paid dearly for it. The benefit of being a captain and in charge of the patrol was being able to keep some of the booty for the team. The general had given him this six-pack of beer as a housewarming gift when he moved in.

He finished the first bottle in seconds and grabbed another. He made an effort to savor this one a little longer. The liquid had a rejuvenating affect, but he knew it would be short-lived. Before long, the brew would work together with his exhaustion and bring him crashing down. He had to be on the floor below before that happened.

He found an old canvas backpack in his closet and filled it with the remaining two bottles, his last bottle of water, and two colas. He added an apple and a small brick of cheddar cheese, then searched the cupboards until he found a box of crackers and a jar of peanut butter. It wasn't much; in fact, he didn't have much, but it would seem like a feast once he got to Melody.

With the second beer finished, Evan went back to the balcony and stepped over the rail. The climb was more difficult and dangerous in the dark, but he didn't want to risk turning the flashlight on. With any luck, the crits would move on if they didn't see him. Otherwise, getting back down was going to be near impossible.

His toes stretched for the rail of the second floor. His arms ached from the exertion. He would not be able to hold out for long. If he didn't find a perch soon, he would have to risk swinging blindly to the platform, hoping he cleared the rail.

He was about to start arching his body to pick up speed, when something grabbed his foot. Startled he pulled away, but the hand gripped him again. He lifted his other foot to deliver a kick when Melody said, "Stop! I'm trying to guide you to the rail."

He relaxed and allowed her to place his foot. The relief was instant. His arms felt like weights had been tied to his hands. He jumped down and the two stood looking at each other for a long, uncomfortable moment. "I told you I'd come back," he said. She rushed forward, wrapping her arms around him, and hugged him tight. He put his hands on her back with as soft a touch as he could manage. "Hey, I brought dinner."

"That's good. This place didn't have much food."

"Oh, so you already ate without me?" he said, hoping his voice sounded as teasing as he intended.

"That's what you get for leaving me behind."

He paused. "Melody, I'm truly sorry."

"I know."

"You wouldn't have survived up there. I barely survived."

"I heard. It sounded pretty intense."

"Believe me, it was."

"You were right. I'm sorry I was being such a pain."

"I'm sorry I gave you such pain."

Her hand probed the back of her head. "Yeah, my head's sore."

"I don't know what came over me. Please forgive me."

"That'll depend on what you brought me for dinner."

He smiled. "Let's go find out."

They sat at the dining room table. Evan spread out the fare. "Help yourself. Take what you like. I'll eat what's left."

She stood and went to the kitchen, returning with a butter knife, a partial loaf of bread, and a jar of jelly. She'd been busy exploring while he was gone. They ate in silence. After a long drink of cola, Melody released a loud belch.

"Pig," Evan said, then let loose one of his own.

"Guess I'm in the right company."

And for the first time since the invasion, he barked out an honest laugh.

When they were finished, they stowed the remains in the backpack. "You can have the bed. I'll sleep here on the couch."

She gave the hall a tentative look. Evan switched on the flashlight and led her to the bedroom. He checked the room while she stood in the doorway. "It's all clear. Sleep well." As he moved past her, she reached out and hugged him again. A pang of guilt and sorrow touched his heart. The poor girl had been through a lot. She'd most likely be through even more before the ordeal was safely behind them. "We'll be all right."

"But," she squeezed tighter, "what about my mom? Will I ever see her again?"

Evan didn't know what to say. He settled on a vague truth. "I don't know. I hope so. We'll see what we find in the morning."

"You promised, remember?"

"I will try, but if we don't see her right away, I'm going to get you to safety with the others and then I'll go looking. Okay?'

She didn't respond.

"Melody, this is important. Please don't fight me. Finding your mother won't do you any good if you end up dead, or worse."

"Okay. But you will look for her?"

"Yes." He pushed her gently away. "Now, get some sleep. I want to leave as soon as the sun comes up."

Evan went back to the front room. The simple effort of sitting on the couch was a strain, but brought instant relief to his aching muscles. He rubbed his face with vigorous strokes before lying down. He tried to shut his mind off, but it battled with exhaustion for control. As sleep began to overtake him, a soft footfall snapped him upright, his hand on the gun.

Melody came into the room carrying a pillow and dragging a blanket and comforter. She spread the comforter on the floor, lay down, and pulled the blanket over her. The whites of her eyes shone at him. "Good night," she said.

"Good night."

36

"Mom!"

The shrill voice pierced his dark dreams, jolting him to a sitting position. Evan scanned the room in confusion. Then the voice cried out again. "No! What are you doing? Mom!"

Evan turned to see Melody leaning over the rail, straining to reach something below. *Mom? Oh shit!* A bolt of anxiety had him on his feet and racing to the young girl. The sun had peeked over the horizon, revealing everything below. On the street, one of Welsh's lackeys ran, carrying a female body over his shoulder. He set the woman on her feet about twenty yards from the horde of crits that had gathered around the first floor balcony.

Evan glanced down and saw they had taken notice and were now moving toward Melody's mom. The frightened Joan looked up at Melody, her eyes wide and white. Then on what was advancing toward her, and she screamed. She turned and tried to get away, but she could only take short hops because her legs had been taped together. Her hands also had been bound and hung uselessly in front of her.

Movement beyond the woman drew Evan's attention. Welsh and his group were making a run for the gate in the fence that bordered the river. He held something in his hand. Of course, the man would have keys to get to his own yacht. The woman screamed again. *Son of a bitch!* Just as he'd suspected, Welsh was using her as a decoy—drawing the crits in their path to her, sacrificing her life for theirs. Before he realized he had done it, the gun was in his hand and firing at Welsh. The range was a bit far for accuracy, but the bullets struck close enough to make all of them duck.

Melody tugged at his arm, making it impossible for him to shoot. "Help her!" she pleaded, her face a tear-streaked mess. Burying his rage at Welsh, Evan threw a leg over the rail and quickly dropped to the first floor balcony. With the crits now advancing toward Melody's mother, Evan was able to leap to the ground unnoticed. He drew the gun and knife and took off at a run.

Not wanting to waste time the woman didn't have, Evan attacked the creatures, dodging between them like an impatient rush hour driver. As he got close and the circle of crits was tighter, he chose to run over them rather than go around. By the time he reached the frantic woman, several undead had grabbed her. She tripped and toppled to the ground, landing hard.

Evan lined up a shot to the back of a thin crit man's head and blew a hole through to the front of its skull. He slashed, kicked, and fired until he was next to her. Squatting, he fired in rapid succession to give himself some room, then risked a glance at the dazed woman. "Don't move!" he shouted, then slid the knife between her legs. Pulling upward, he severed the tape, but in his haste, only half of it split.

Hands touched his and grabbed at the knife. He pulled away until he saw it was her. Their eyes met briefly and Evan released the blade to her. He turned, pulled out a magazine and fired until the one in the gun was empty. He slapped a new one home and glanced down. Her legs were free, but she was trying to invert the blade to cut through the binds on her hands. There was no time. He had to get her moving. He reached down, snagged the tape around her wrists and hauled her to her feet.

"We have to move." He took the knife. "Run toward the buses."

She hesitated. He fired four times and shoved her to get her started. She ran as Evan gave her cover. They gained some distance, but as he moved, he became aware of shouting. He looked around for the source, stopping on the balcony where a large portion of the group was yelling and pointing downward. He followed their motions and saw Melody trying to duck around four crits. A dangling cable told him all he needed to know. She had climbed down on her own.

Without a second's hesitation, Evan bolted for her. She ducked and disappeared from sight as the creatures closed around her. Evan shot on the run, aiming high. His first two missed, but the third ripped into the back of a tall head. The body toppled into the circle, his shielding Melody from the others for the moment. With an opening now, she began crawling away.

Evan pulled up five feet short, and in a smooth, systematic sweep, he eliminated the immediate threat. He stretched a hand down to Melody without taking his eyes from the pursuit. She took it and he helped her up. "Run to your mother." She didn't wait for further orders or encouragement.

Evan backed away from the advancing crits to protect her retreat. He gave her two seconds before turning to follow. As he did, he looked up and motioned with his arm "Come on!"

A few of the elite men had already begun descending. His thoughts flicked to Welsh and the yachts. He had to stop them before they escaped. Seeing Melody and Joan in front of him, locked in an embrace, he pushed it away. First he had to get them to safety.

He yelled for them to climb, but they looked at him and didn't move. He reached them and shouted. "Melody, climb up the bumper. Go." He turned his attention to her mother. Her hands were still taped together and she would need assistance. He slid the knife into its sheath, then he whipped her around so she was facing the bus, then placed a hand on each hip and lifted her. She let out a squeal of surprise, but was able to get her feet on the bumper.

Melody had already scampered up and was on the hood, looking down. "Melody, help your mother." He got behind her as she tried to get a leg up on the hood. Placing both hands beneath her butt, he pushed upward. She rose high enough for Melody to grab her hands and pull. Once safely on the hood, Evan was quick to follow.

He slid the knife free and handed it to Melody. "Cut your mother free, then climb up the windshield to the roof and wait there for the others to arrive." He didn't look to see if she followed his directions. His focus was now elsewhere. He ran up the steeply-sloped windshield, and gaining the roof, began running toward the fence while scanning for Welsh and company. His gaze stopped at the boathouse, noting one of the doors stood open.

As Evan reached the end of the bus, he remembered the four-foot gap that existed between the last bus and the fence. Instead of stopping, he increased his speed, pushed off the bus and went airborne. He extended his feet in front of him like an Olympic long jumper and cleared the eight-foot-high fence. Landing in a squat on the sandy of the beach, he rolled, hands and knees stopping his momentum, then shot forward toward the long pier.

A man came out of the open boathouse door, his head down and looking at a ring of keys. He stopped outside the second boathouse door and inserted one of them. Evan couldn't let him get inside where he could lock the door between them, but with thirty yards to the dock and another hundred feet of pier to get down, it didn't seem likely.

He pushed himself harder, but running on sand did not make for good speed. Three more people came out of the first door and joined the man. As the second door swung open, Evan raised the gun and snapped off two shots in their direction. The bullets impacted against the aluminum structure above their heads. They ducked. A man and woman ran back to the first door and pulled it shut behind them. The other man and woman stepped through the opening and swung the other door closed.

Evan swore. Lowering the gun, he pumped his arms hard to gain extra speed. A boat engine roared to life, but Evan couldn't tell which boathouse it had come from. He hit the pier, his footfalls pounding loud and hard, making the panels beneath him sway with the contact. He had a choice to make and decided on the boathouse to the right. They had less time to get underway there.

The tone of the engine changed as if it had been put into

gear. Evan envisioned the yachts pulling away from their berths. He reached the building and veered to the right. The door was locked, but it was only aluminum and he figured it should give, but as he thundered a kick just below the handle, the frame dented, but did not move. Then he heard the second engine fire. *No!* He couldn't allow both of them to get away.

37

He took three long strides to the end of boathouse and dove off the pier. He reacted so fast that he still had a grip on the gun. The water was dark and he had to swim blind. Two strokes later, his hand collided with a support post, sending a dull pain up his arm. Evan kept going, using shadows and light to guide him. He moved toward the water that was away from the shadow of the boathouse and muscled his way through the water.

As he came up for air, he discovered he was at the side of the second yacht; however, it was moving backward. He paddled harder, as if the water was his opponent in a fight. He had to reach the swimming platform off the bow, but as the large boat continued in reverse, Evan knew he would never make it in time. A louder engine rumbled across the water, announcing that the first yacht was already underway.

He had to stop this one. With every bit of strength he possessed, he pulled the oar through the water, but his efforts were in vain. He couldn't gain ground on the yacht. Then he caught a break. The yacht turned across his path to face down river. Stroke after stroke brought him closer, and with each one, his hope grew. Then the pilot shifted gears. The large craft began to move forward.

Still, Evan had one chance. Not allowing the disappointment to slow him down, he angled forward. As the tall white hull slid past his eyes, he drew ever closer. The wooden swimming platform was now in full view. Ten feet. He propelled onward. Five feet, and he was even with the platform. He had only seconds to make a stab at it. He risked another stroke, then lunged through the water, trying to latch on to anything.

His fingers snagged between the water slits in the last board. He dug in and held on as the yacht slowly picked up speed. He pulled until his chest rested on the platform. Sucking air, he muscled his legs up, then crawled, flopping his exhausted body down.

Valuable seconds passed and the yacht moved farther from the shore. Evan forced himself to stand. The gun was still in his hand, but he had no idea if it would fire. It should, he told himself, but maybe the pilot would be persuaded to turn around by the mere sight of it pointed at him—if it was even possible with a boat this big.

He reached the ladder and climbed, one rung at a time, until his head rose high enough to peer over the gunwale. Both occupants had their backs to him, their attention focused on the yacht ahead. A sudden tightening of the woman's shoulders gave Evan sign of her intent to turn around. As her head began to swivel, Evan ducked. He held his breath as if she could hear it over the roar of the engine. He waited for a fifty count before inching upward.

The pilot increased the speed again. A quick look behind showed Evan the pier was fast receding. He had to act, and now. In a burst, he climbed up and stepped down on the deck. The motion of the yacht threw him off balance. He reached for the support of a bench and the gun smacked loudly. Gaining his sea legs, Evan looked up to see the woman staring at him, wide-eyed. She tugged on the man's arm and spoke to him.

Evan advanced on shaky legs as the man turned. He raised the gun. "You will turn this vessel around, or I will shoot you and drop you in the river."

The man and woman stared at each other, speechless. Evan wanted very badly to place an encouraging shot over their heads, but was afraid the gun wouldn't fire. Instead, he walked forward and leveled the gun at the man's face. "I oughta shoot you right now for what you did."

"That wasn't us," the woman squealed, lowering herself into a squat, as if being smaller would protect her from a bullet.

"That's right," the man offered, raising his hands in front

of his face. "It was all Welsh's idea. We didn't want to hurt anyone."

"And yet, you went along with him. You couldn't even leave this boat knowing there were still people back there."

"I-I, we, uh, ..."

Evan saw red. His finger tightened on the trigger, wanting very much to blow the man away. He stepped forward, swatting the man's hands aside. Placing the barrel square on the man's forehead, he said, "Last chance. Turn this thing around, or you're dead."

"Please don't. I'll do it," he whined. Evan stepped back and noticed a large wet spot spreading along the front of the man's pants. He turned to the wheel. The woman sat down, covered her face, and cried.

Suddenly, the deck beneath Evan shifted and he flew sideways. He hit the side wall of the cabin. The gun went flying and the man lunged for it, leaving the wheel. Evan reacted with desperate quickness. He jumped to his feet and went after the man. The pilot reached the gun first, but Evan was right behind and landed on his back, driving him face first to the deck.

As they struggled, a weight fell on Evan's back. Nails raked at his eyes. A long, burning scratch gouged into his cheek less than an inch from his right eye. Evan snapped his head backward into the woman's face. She shrieked and fell away. The man got his feet underneath him and tried to stand up. He had both hands around the gun and a superior position over Evan.

Evan drove his feet into the deck, propelling the man forward. They smacked in to the opposite wall and bounced back, the impact causing Evan to slip. He dropped to his knees, but kept his grip on his opponent. Evan dragged the man back to the floor like a wrestler performing a takedown. They landed on top of the woman, who was writhing on the deck with her hands cupped over her bloody nose.

Evan grabbed the man's hair with both hands and drove his face onto the wood. He bounced him twice, then released with his right hand and drove his fist into the woman's cupped hands. She groaned and went still.

The man, though less active, stretched his hands over his head and out of Evan's reach, trying to turn the gun at an angle that would shoot back at Evan. Somehow, he managed to get the barrel around and yanked on the trigger. The explosion shocked them both, and they cried out in unison. The bullet passed inches from Evan's face. At least now he knew the gun worked.

Evan slid to the side as the next round went off. Choosing to go for the face instead of the gun, Evan jammed his finger into the man's eye. The reaction was immediate. He screamed and went wild, swinging his body back and forth to break free. When he let go of the gun with one hand to pull Evan's fingers away, Evan dove for the gun. In one motion, he ripped it from the man's hand with a *snap*, followed by another scream.

Evan stood and aimed the gun at the man. Before he pulled the trigger, he looked up to see the yacht was on a collision course with a small island. With his heart in his throat, he dove for the wheel. He spun hard and grabbed the throttle, yanking it back. The vessel pitched hard to the right. Evan had to hold on to keep from being thrown.

With great effort, he succeeded in guiding the yacht past the island, but something bumped beneath them. The yacht seemed to go airborne for an instant before slamming down. He prayed the hull hadn't been breached. He shifted into neutral to let the vessel settle down and his heart stop thumping. As an afterthought, he looked around for the man and woman. He found her body sprawled under a bench. She wasn't moving. He didn't care to find out if she were alive or dead. He could not find the man. Had he gotten up and fled for a safe haven somewhere below decks? He was too tired to search for him now. Besides, the others would be going into panic mode. He needed to get back.

38

Evan maneuvered the yacht back and forth and few times before getting her nose headed in the right direction. Breathing easier now, he looked down the river. Something splashed wildly just ahead. He leaned forward and narrowed his eyes to get a better look. He discovered the man floundering in the water. He must have gotten thrown over during one of Evan's sudden moves.

Ha! Serves him right. But even after all the man had done, Evan couldn't bring himself to abandon another living person. He slowed and stopped close to the bobbing man. He searched the benches and cupboards for a rope. Finding one, he went to the side and readied to pitch the line to the man, but he was no longer in sight. He scanned the area, coming up empty, and then decided he didn't care that much about him, either.

Replacing the rope, Evan pushed the lever into gear and throttled up. He arrived back at the pier to find a small group had already gathered, while others were still climbing down or crossing the buses. Evan turned the yacht around again and idled at the end of a pier down one from the dual boathouses. He hopped to the dock and tied off, then went to help the others. Almost off the dock, he had a second thought and went back. He shut the engine off and pocketed the key. No sense in taking any chances that someone else might be anxious to leave without the rest of them.

Approaching the fence, Evan saw someone had broken the legs off a dining room table and balanced it between the bus and the fence to bridge the gap. It was a good idea. He slowed, searching for Teke. She was not in the group already over the fence. Six people had crossed and were busy helping others over. She was most likely bringing up the rear. Helen and Jack were at the fence now, waiting for assistance. He stepped aside to get a better look down the long line of escapees moving over the tops of the buses. He still could not see her. Evan became anxious.

A few people were still on the balcony waiting their turn to mount the buses. Teke was not there either. A growing wall of crits lined the buses on both sides. They reached upward, trying to snare anything that moved. The bodies in front were being smashed against the buses as more undead arrived and pressed forward.

Evan switched his search to finding Ervin. The big man was nearing the end of the second bus. He and another man named Darby carried a blanket between them, a body slung within. *Teke!* He knew it was her without being able to see her. *What had happened?*

Evan jumped on the fence and began climbing. He reached the crossbar just as Ervin and Darby came to the first sloping windshield. Darby started down, but the angle was too steep for him as he was trying to keep the blanket level. He tripped and fell, his body rolling off the hood. He screamed as his feet dangled within range of a group of crits. Excitement ignited movement throughout the crowd as the creatures made a mad press forward to get at him.

Evan was a blur of motion, leaping to the table, almost bouncing Helen into the waiting horde. He gripped her, holding her until she regained her balance, then leaped for the bus, his eyes focusing hard on Teke. With the blanket now lying along the slope of the windshield, her body began to slide. The first thing Evan noticed was that she was not trying to prevent her drop. Her eyes were closed and Evan realized she was unconscious.

He tried to move faster, but others were crossing and he had to be cautious he didn't knock them off the roof. Ahead, all hell was breaking loose. People reached down to pull the Darby up, but they were in a life or death tug-of-war battle with the crits who held his legs. Ervin dropped to his knees and stretched his long frame for Teke, but she had slid too far. As her feet touched the hood, her body twisted. She rolled down the windshield to the hood, her head now at the edge and hanging over.

Filthy, disease-ridden fingers reached for her. To his extreme horror, he saw a taller creature catch a handful of her hair and begin to drag her backward. A gun barked, drawing a hopeful Evan's attention. Ervin was trying to do a controlled slide down the windshield while firing into the crowd. Teke's descent was slowed for a moment, but now she hung within reach of several others who latched on and drew her down faster than before.

Gorge rising, Evan reached the end of the bus and began firing at random, so panicked for Teke's safety that he gave no thought to accuracy. He ran down the windshield and stood on the hood, blasting away.

"Grab her!" he yelled to Ervin. The big man bent and stretched out. Meanwhile, Darby was being dragged down, his team losing the battle for his body. He reached for Evan. "Help me!" Evan was torn. To help him, he had to stop firing, which made saving Teke less likely. The man screamed as he lost his hold on the grill.

With lightning reactions, Evan dove for Darby, latching on with one hand and firing point-blank into the tops of the heads of the crits nearest to him. The gun emptied. Two other men joined him and grabbed an arm. Evan had to release his grip to change out magazines. In an instant, he was firing again.

The two men began winning the fight and were able to pull Darby to safety. Without waiting to see if they made it, Evan leaped to the hood of the abutted bus. Ervin had managed to get Teke pulled back, but his frame was so long, his legs hung over the opposite side. He was being pulled backward despite his strength and best efforts.

Evan dragged Teke back another six inches to ensure she was out of reach, then he sat on Ervin's back to add weight and methodically blew away any foul creature that had a grip on his legs. When he was free, Ervin drew his legs up and lay on his back, panting hard and staring at the cloudless morning sky.

"Come on, Ervin. The others need our help." He offered a hand and the big man took it. Once on his feet, he placed a hand on Evan's shoulder. "Thanks. I thought I was done for."

Evan nodded. "We need to get everyone to the other side." He looked back and saw the fallen man was being helped over the fence. Behind them, a line of twelve people waited for Ervin and Evan to move.

"Let's get Teke over, then come back to help." Ervin nodded. He looked at the gathering group watching them from the roof. "Wait here. We'll be back to help you."

As they repositioned her on the blanket, Evan said, "What's wrong with her?"

"She's got a fever. Doc says her wound's infected, but she didn't have anything to give her to fight it."

Evan reached into his pocket and fingered the baggie holding the antibiotics. *Would they help? Would they be enough? Would it be in time?* He looked down at her and wiped strands of hair away from her sweaty face. A lump formed in his throat. They had to work. He couldn't lose her. Not now. Not after everything they'd been through.

"Come on, Evan. The others are waiting."

They bent, grabbed two corners each and lifted the blanket. Carefully, they stepped from hood to hood, then at the windshield, Evan lowered her as Ervin held her in place. He then scaled the glass. Once on the roof, he reached and lifted her up. Again they set her down while Ervin climbed up. From there, they reached the fence and lowered her with care to others on the ground. Evan extended his hand holding the pills to the doctor. "I found these. Will they help?"

She took them and read the label. "Not perfect, but better than nothing. I'll get them into her now."

Evan stood. Ervin was looking down at his legs. He looked up with an expression of relief. "Whew! Had me worried for a moment."

Evan offered a tight smile. He hadn't checked his own leg and didn't want to, but the flesh burned. He wondered how long he had left. He pushed the thought from his mind. They had others to save.

Ervin started to move, but Evan grabbed his arm. "Best to reload right now, rather than run out when we need it." They loaded all magazines, then moved back to where the two bus grills touched. They stood opposite each other on the hoods, creating a channel for those crossing to pass between. They helped them down and back up, one at a time.

Once everyone had crossed, they followed. At the fence, Evan shoved the table back on the roof to prevent the crits from climbing on the buses. He didn't want to drop it to the ground so the other survivors could still climb to safety. With a final look back at the tower, he jumped to the ground.

39

Evan led them down the dock. Before he allowed them to board, he said, "We have too many people for a boat this size, but like I told you before, we aren't leaving anyone behind. Once aboard, you need to get situated and as comfortable as you can. I'm not sure how long we'll be on the water before we can find a safe place to dock, but I hope it won't be too long. Continue to help each other. It's the only reason we've survived so far."

"Any idea where we'll go?" a woman asked.

"I really don't know. We can discuss that once everyone is aboard."

A rattling sound drew all their attention to the fence. To Evan's surprise, several of the crits were attempting to climb. One, having gained the hood of a bus, was trying to claw its way up the steep windshield, but kept sliding backwards. It was yet another sign to him that the crits were morphing into something more intelligent. If that were truly the case, they would be even more dangerous.

Keeping his voice calm, he said, "We need to go now. Watch your step."

It took them more than thirty minutes to get everyone situated. Once he was sure everyone was safe, Evan started the engines and throttled up. As the yacht began to move, he glanced toward the fence. Several of the creatures had reached the top. One lost its balance and fell over, landing in a puff of sand. *Damn!*

He looked ahead and thought about Teke. The doctor had crushed two pills and forced them down her throat. All she could do was offer hope that they would do some good to at least break the fever. Otherwise, she shrugged, but left it there.

Ervin and a more-rejuvenated Jack came to stand with

him. "So where to, Captain?" Jack said with a smile.

Evan shrugged. "I have no idea. If either of you have any thoughts, let's hear them."

Jack said, "Not far from here, just around the peninsula there," he pointed to a promontory jutting into the channel, "Is a large shipping dock. There's a lot of warehouses and the area is fenced. It might not do for a permanent solution, but it might serve until we can regroup."

"Sounds good to me. You know how to handle one of these?"

Jack smiled. "Oh yeah."

Evan handed him the key. "Have at it, Captain."

While Jack moved to get the vessel underway, Ervin said, "What about Welsh?"

That was a good question.

"Are we going to just let him get away with what he did?"

"For now, I don't see that we have much choice," Evan replied. "Our safety is the first concern. But we'll find him again, and when we do, he's gonna pay."

"Yeah," Ervin said. "He's definitely gonna to pay."

They cruised until near sunset, as "just around the peninsula" was farther than advertised. Jack docked, but before he allowed anyone to disembark, he led a small group to inspect the perimeter to make sure the fence was intact.

They led the group to one of the smaller warehouses. There, the injured were examined and the meager food rations were distributed. While the party ate and then collapsed into an exhausted silence, Evan went to check on Teke.

He sat next to her and stroked her hair. The doctor came over a few minutes later to check on her. Checking her temperature, she lifted an eyebrow in mild surprise. "Her fever's down a degree. It's not much at this point, but we'll watch and hope." She placed another crushed pill under Teke's tongue. "It's not the best way to do this, but since she's unconscious, there's really no other way."

She sat down next to Evan and leaned in close, lowering

her voice. "We do have a problem, though."

Thinking she meant with Teke, Evan swallowed hard. "Darby." The doctor nodded toward the man they had rescued on the bus. "He has several bites on his legs. The area isn't infected now, but if it becomes infected, I'm not sure what I can do for him, other than amputate. If the infection is in him already, even that severe measure might be too late. Without a proper medical facility, he'll die anyway."

Evan nodded his understanding. He closed his eyes and leaned his head back against the wall. Christ, it never ended. Their numbers were diminishing, and for some reason, the number of crits seemed to be increasing. "How long do you think?"

"Not sure, but I'd guess maybe two to three days."

"Okay, Doc. Thanks for telling me. And please, don't mention this to anyone else. At least not yet. I'd like them to have a feeling of safety and security, at least for the time being. They could use a day or two without any stress."

"I understand. How do you want to handle it, you know, if..."

"If he turns?" Evan was annoyed by the question. What did the woman want from him?

"Yeah."

"There's only one way to deal with it, Doc."

The doctor didn't respond. She sighed, stood and left Evan to his thoughts.

Evan closed his eyes, but seconds later, they snapped open. He looked down at his leg. With slow movements, as if he were straining against an unseen force, he reached for his pant leg. His fingers wrapped around the cuff. He hesitated, exhaling. Sucking his breath in and holding it, he pulled the pant leg up a few inches, and then he saw the dried blood on his sock.

He stopped and blew out his breath in a long, steady stream, like a balloon with a pinhole leak. Without looking any farther, he pulled the fabric back down. How much time did *he* have? He rested for a while, not thinking about his situation. He'd already made the decision. Now, it was time to rest. He needed to regain some strength.

Later that night while everyone slept, Evan crept to where Ervin had crashed. He nudged the big man and covered his mouth with a hand, putting a finger to his lips. When Ervin nodded, he released him and motioned for him to follow. They went outside and walked away from the warehouse.

Evan hunched his shoulders in a defeated gesture. After everything he'd done to get them all to safety, he'd lost in the end. The evening had taken on a chill, or perhaps he was merely feeling the effects of his decision and his upcoming fate. "Ervin, I'm going back to see if I can find any other survivors."

"What? Already?"

"I can't wait because they can't wait. I have to go now."

"I'll go with you."

"No," he said sharply. He softened his voice. "No, they're going to need you and Jack and the doc to get them to wherever you're going to go. Leave a message here for whoever follows. Try to leave clues along the way if you move on."

"But you can't do this alone."

"I'm the only one who can. I'll not risk anyone else's life. It's for the best. You keep the gun, but I want one more magazine. I'll load them up and leave you the remaining bullets. I should be able to find replacements once I get back inside."

"What should I tell Teke?"

Suddenly, Evan was unable to speak. His eyes watered and his throat went dry. He swallowed hard a few times to try to remove the lump. "Tell her—tell her I'm sorry."

Ervin let the silence grow as he studied Evan's face. "There's something else going on here, isn't there? What is it? You're not coming back, are you?"

Again, the words were too hard to speak. He turned away and the tears fell. He wiped at them and turned to face his friend. "I've been bitten."

"Oh God, Evan."

"I don't know how long I have. But I'm not going to stay here and wait to change. As long as I can still function, I'm going to do something. I'll find any other survivors and get them out. I don't expect to be coming back."

Silence.

"Evan, I don't know what to say. I'm sorry."

"Don't tell anyone, please. I'd rather they remember me like this. And if... and when Teke wakes, tell her...I love her."

"When are you going?"

"Now."

Ervin reached into a back pocket and produced a magazine. Evan took it from him and slipped it into his own pocket. He took the remaining bullets out of his pouch and handed the boxes to Ervin. The big man took them, clasping both hands around Evan's. "It's been an honor. Good luck and God bless."

Evan gave a half smile, turned and walked away into the darkness. At the fence, he looked back over his shoulder, but he couldn't see anything. He climbed and dropped to the other side. He was on his own now, for however long it would be.

He set a brisk pace, afraid to take too long. He feared the disease might manifest before he was able to complete his mission. As he walked, he pushed all thoughts of the group and Teke from his mind and began forming his plan. He had a lot of ground to cover, and quickly. He could do this. He refused to feel sorry for himself and his inevitable end, knowing he would eat a bullet long before becoming a monster, providing they hadn't already taken him down. In his line of work in this strange world, this end had always been a possibility. It was an accepted part of the job, although in truth, he never thought it would happen to him.

He let his thoughts turn to Teke. To her smile, her laugh and that kiss, and for a while, he was happy.

Made in the USA
Middletown, DE
07 February 2025

70328045R00116